ROB

THE SOCCER MAD DOUBLE

including

FOOTBALL FLUKES
FOOTBALL DAFT

Illustrated by Aidan Potts

CORGI YEARLING BOOKS

THE SOCCER MAD DOUBLE
A CORGI YEARLING BOOK : 0 440 864488

First publication in Great Britain

PRINTING HISTORY
This Collection first published 2000

1 3 5 7 9 10 8 6 4 2

Collection copyright © Rob Childs, 2000

includes

FOOTBALL FLUKES
First published in Great Britain by Corgi Yearling Books, 1997
Copyright © Rob Childs, 1997
Illustrations copyright © Aidan Potts, 1997

FOOTBALL DAFT
First published in Great Britain by Corgi Yearling Books, 1997
Copyright © Rob Childs, 1997
Illustrations copyright © Aidan Potts, 1997

The lines on pages 28, 47 and 112 of *Football Flukes* are extracts from the poem
If by Rudyard Kipling; reproduced by permission of A P Watt Ltd on behalf of the
National Trust

The right of Rob Childs to be identified as the author of this work has been
asserted in accordance with the Copyright, Designs and Patents Act 1988

Set in 12/15pt Linotype Century Schoolbook by
Phoenix Typesetting, Ilkley, West Yorkshire

Corgi Yearling Books are published by Transworld Publishers,
61–63 Uxbridge Road, London W5 5SA,
a division of The Random House Group Ltd,
in Australia by Random House Australia (Pty) Ltd,
20 Alfred Street, Milsons Point, Sydney, NSW 2061, Australia,
in New Zealand by Random House New Zealand Ltd,
18 Poland Road, Glenfield, Auckland 10, New Zealand
and in South Africa by Random House (Pty) Ltd,
Endulini, 5a Jubilee Road, Parktown 2193, South Africa

Made and printed in Great Britain by
Cox & Wyman Ltd, Reading, Berkshire

ROB CHILDS

FOOTBALL FLUKES

ILLUSTRATED BY
AIDAN POTTS

For soccer's underdogs – dream on and may
your team be lucky!

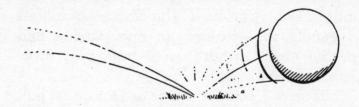

1   Cup Trail

'We're on our way to Wembley! We're on our way to Wembley! La-la-la-la! La-la-la-la!'

The hopeful chant might have carried greater conviction if dozens of travelling supporters were rocking the coach with their delirious optimism. As it was, a few off-key, croaky voices from the back of an old van didn't have quite the same effect. Even if they did belong to the actual players.

'Quit that racket, will you!' the driver ordered. 'I'm trying to concentrate on where I'm going. And it certainly isn't Wembley.'

'Are we nearly there yet, Dad?' Luke chirped up, undeterred.

Mr Crawford sighed. 'You've already asked me that twice in the last ten minutes. I'm still none the wiser. Ray's got the map.'

'Bet he's got no idea how to find this place either,' Sanjay grunted. The goalkeeper rubbed a gap in the steamed-up, rear window and peered out. 'I'm sure we've been past these houses before.'

Luke saw Uncle Ray's crowded estate car pull into the kerb without warning, causing his dad to brake suddenly and jerk his own passengers against their seat-belts. The car behind, the third member of their little football convoy, almost ran into the back of them. All three drivers got out and began a heated argument over the map in the middle of the road, involving much shaking of heads and gesticulating.

Luke consulted his watch anxiously. 'We should be there by now. It's almost kick-off time.'

'The match can't start without us, can it?' said Titch, squeezed in between Sanjay and Tubs. It was a squash even for someone as pint-sized as Titch. Tubs's vast backside took up most of the long seat.

The full-back's rumbling laugh now filled the

van too. 'I wouldn't be too sure about that. It's gonna be so one-sided, I don't suppose they'd notice whether we turned up or not.'

'Rubbish!' countered Luke vehemently. 'They'll know they've got a game on their hands once we get stuck into them. The cup's got our name on it this year, I can feel it.'

'At the rate we're going, I'd tell the engraver to make it next year, if I were you,' Sanjay observed dryly.

Luke decided it was time to take action. 'If you want a job doing properly, do it yourself,' he muttered, climbing out of the van to stop a passer-by and ask directions to the local park.

Luke did most things himself as far as his Under-13 Sunday League team were concerned. Not only was he captain of Swillsby Swifts, he was coach, trainer and player-manager too. Picking the side was the only way Luke could guarantee getting a game each week.

The three men returned sheepishly to their vehicles and the convoy trundled on – just fifty metres to the half-concealed park entrance. They were greeted, for want of a better word, by the impatient, short-tempered team manager of Digby Dynamos.

'You lot are so late, I've got every right to claim a walk-over through to the next round,' he fumed, brandishing the League's handbook at them. 'That's what the rules say in here, y'know.'

Luke's dad attempted to apologize, but the man was in no mood to listen to any excuses. He turned on his heel with a parting sneer. 'Good job for you my lads still want to play. They're out to break the club record today for the number of goals scored in a single match!'

'Right, men. All ready?' Luke demanded once the Swifts had changed.

'Ready, Skipper,' they responded dutifully, out of habit, humouring Luke's favourite rallying cry before they took the field.

'Remember, win this and we're in the last sixteen,' he beamed. 'We're on the cup trail!'

'Up a cul-de-sac, more like,' grunted Big Ben, their gangling centre-back. 'Reckon we've got more chance of winning the Lottery!'

Luke refused to tolerate any pessimism. 'You've got to be in to win. And we still are, thanks to our great victory in the first round.'

'That was a fluke and you know it. Lightning doesn't strike twice.'

'The skipper might be right for once,' Tubs cut in, making heads turn towards him in disbelief. They didn't know which notion was more weird. The idea of Luke being right, or Tubs supporting him.

'I mean, we *are* the strongest team in the League,' Tubs continued, struggling to keep a straight face. 'We're bottom of the table, holding everybody else up!'

'That's an old joke,' Luke retorted as Tubs's loud rumbles echoed around the bare changing room. 'League positions count for nothing in the cup. This is a one-off game. C'mon, let's get at 'em!'

The Swifts, still giggling, trotted out in their new all-gold strip with its bright green logo on the front of the shirts: GREAT GAME!

The kit was about the only thing they had won all season so far. Luke had showed off his un-rivalled knowledge of football trivia in a soccer magazine competition to earn the star prize for his team. It was just a shame the Swifts weren't so hot on the pitch.

This morning, they were really caught cold. The Dynamos had been warming up for twenty minutes, increasingly annoyed at being kept waiting. Now they were like dogs suddenly let off the leash, tearing around the field, chasing and snapping at everything that moved. There seemed to be twice as many red shirts on the pitch as gold, and Luke's dad had to convince himself otherwise. He counted them to make sure.

Unbelievably, the Swifts' goal remained intact, adding to the home team's frustrations. Sanjay's superstitious habit before the kick-off of jumping up to touch the crossbar to bring him luck appeared for once to be working. At least, the goalkeeper thought so. Everything he missed clanged against the metal frame or flew wide of the target, as if the ball had forgotten the magic password to gain entrance into the sacred net.

Sanjay's grin broadened as another shot cannoned off his shoulder and looped up over the bar. He gave the striker a little smirk. 'Guess it's not your day, eh, pal?'

'Don't bank on it. We'll have double figures before the end.'

'Should have had them by now,' scowled the Dynamos' captain. 'C'mon, guys. Their luck can't last out much longer. Once we get the first, the floodgates will open.'

The Swifts' skipper of course didn't see it like that at all. But then Luke's rose-tinted view of the game was always different to everyone else's. As usual, he broadcast it to the world as he charged madly around after the ball, trying in vain to get a kick. It was not so much a running commentary as a stop-start, puff and pant one.

15

'Another great save by Sanjay Mistry, the Swifts' courageous custodian. He saw the ball late but got his body well behind it to concede the corner. Skipper Luke Crawford now organizes his team's marking at the set-piece, picking up the dangerous number eight himself. The ball swirls over into the goalmouth and . . . Uuuughh!'

The commentary was abruptly cut off as though someone had pulled the plug out of the socket. Luke had been flattened by the number eight's soaring leap for the ball. He felt like he'd been struck by a jumbo jet, but the impact of bodies was just enough to spoil the attacker's aim. The ball shaved a layer of rust off the outside of the upright as it zoomed by.

Not that Luke saw what happened. He was still eating dirt, face down in the six-yard box. He would have appealed for a foul if he'd had any breath left to do so. Or if he could have spat the piece of mud out of his mouth in time.

With the commentator left speechless, it was just as well that the match wasn't being tele-vized live. The only camera on the ground was operated by Uncle Ray, roaming around the touchline. Luke liked to have the Swifts' games videoed in order to study where things had gone wrong. The analysis usually took him a very long time.

'Think I'll edit this bit out,' Luke decided, looking as if he'd just dunked his face into a vat of molten chocolate. It didn't taste like it.

Sanjay's goal was kept so much under siege that the Dynamos' keeper was relieving his boredom by leaning on a post and chatting to a couple of friends. He'd only touched the ball twice. And one of those was a hoofed clearance from a sympathetic back-pass to give him something to do.

The next time he had contact with the ball was to pick it, red-faced, out of the back of his net. Distracted by a joke, he failed to appreciate the danger when the visitors' left-winger set off on a meandering dribble. He wished now he'd left hearing the punchline till later.

Brian Draper, Brain to his teammates, was the one player of true quality that the Swifts boasted. Naturally two-footed, Brain's fancy footwork turned his baffled marker inside-out so many times that the boy's knickers must have got into the proverbial twist. Perhaps that was why he finally tripped and fell over, leaving Brain clear to torment somebody else.

The winger's next trick was to perform a perfect nutmeg. He slipped the ball cheekily through another defender's legs, nipped round

him to collect it again and then cut inside for goal.

'Watch out!' screamed the captain to wake up his dreamy goalie. 'He's going to shoot.'

Too late. The shot was already on its way. It wasn't hit with any special power, but the ball curled in a graceful arc towards the far corner of the goal. The keeper scrambled desperately across his line, as if chasing a loose piece of paper in the wind, but he was never going to catch it in time. The net did the job for him.

19

'One-nil!' exulted Luke, making no effort to keep any note of bias out of his commentary. 'A *flash of magic from Brain and the Swifts are ahead. Some people might say it was against the run of play, but who cares? This is the cup! Anything can happen!*'

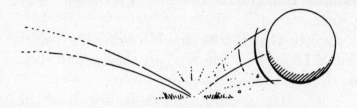

2 We Wuz Robbed!

Nobody in either camp could quite believe the 1–0 half-time scoreline.

Well, nobody except Luke. 'Told you we could win this match,' he enthused during his animated team-talk. 'We've got to hang on to this lead now. Keep a clean sheet and we're through. Concentrate on defence . . .'

The skipper was interrupted as usual. 'We've got no choice. Getting the ball over the halfway line is a major achievement.'

Luke's uncle glanced at the shirt of the speaker. Number three – Gary. Gregg wore

number ten. It was the only way he could tell the identical Garner twins apart. Their father, who had helped with transport, caught his eye and grinned. Ray smiled back, embarrassed, wondering whether Mr Garner himself had similar difficulties knowing which son was which.

Striker Gregg took up his brother's point. 'Yeah, I don't even know where their penalty box is. I've not been in it yet.'

'Just imagine how they're feeling,' cackled Sanjay. 'We've had one shot and scored. Dynamos must have had about a hundred.'

'That's football – you have to take your chances,' Luke said with a shrug. 'Right, second half. Keep it up, men. Good luck!'

'We'll need it,' laughed Gary. 'Let's hope we haven't used it all up.'

Sanjay tried to ensure that they hadn't. He was quick to repeat his 'lucky' routine, jumping up and touching the crossbar of his new goal. And this time he also blew it a kiss for good measure.

The Dynamos kicked off and their bombardment began all over again. Shots and headers rained in at Sanjay from every angle and from inside and outside the penalty area. Some went

22

wide, some over, some were blocked by other players or kicked off the line and scrambled away. He even managed to stop a few himself. Then, with just ten minutes to go, a shot smashed against the underside of the round, metal crossbar.

'*Oohh! What a let off!*' Luke squealed in excitement as his live commentary conveyed the full emotion of the game. '*The ball ricocheted from the bar at ninety degrees, bounced up off the line and now Sanjay's safely pouched it. Dynamos are going berserk, appealing for a goal, but there's no way that went in. No way!*'

The game had to be halted. The referee was quickly surrounded by loud protesters, all insisting that they'd scored.

'C'mon, ref! That was a goal,' cried the Dynamos' captain. 'Anybody could see that.'

'Ball bounced well over the line,' claimed a teammate.

The official's indecision did little to defuse the situation. 'Sorry, I'm not sure that it did,' he faltered. 'It all happened so quickly.'

'Then ask the linesman,' the captain demanded. 'He's got his flag up. Go over and talk to him.'

There was hardly any need to do that. The linesman was making it perfectly plain what his views were. He was jumping up and down, screaming that it was a goal. The referee considered that the linesman's judgement might not exactly be neutral. He was the Dynamos' manager.

'The whole ball has to cross the line, and I can't be certain that it did,' the referee explained to the players. 'I'm giving the goalkeeper the benefit of the doubt. No goal!'

The captain went ballistic! He seemed to lose all self control and gave vent to a whole string of swear words, most of them directed at the

24

referee. Then everybody saw red: the red card that the official drew out of his top pocket and flourished at the boy.

'Off!' he ordered. 'I'm sending you off for using abusive language. You'll be reported to the League and suspended.'

The player was totally gobsmacked. 'You c-can't do that,' he stammered out. 'I'm the captain.'

'It doesn't matter if you're the Archbishop of Canterbury! I'm the ref and I'm in charge. And you're off!'

The man pointed sternly to the changing rooms and the boy's shoulders sagged. He

25

realized he had not only let himself down, but his side too. They were now reduced to ten men. He turned, his lips visibly quivering, and trudged off the field to the stunned silence of his teammates. He didn't want anybody to see his tears.

The drama wasn't over yet. As the captain departed, Luke saw Uncle Ray being led by the arm across the pitch towards them by the Dynamos' manager.

'Take a look at this, ref,' the manager yelled out. 'We've got video evidence here. This'll prove it was a goal!'

'I don't even know if I got a proper shot of it,' Ray was saying, trying not to drop the camcorder into the mud. 'I haven't really got the hang of this thing yet. It's not easy, you know . . .'

'Excuses, excuses. C'mon, ref! Take a butcher's at this film.'

The referee stood firm. 'You can't expect me to stand here and squint at some fuzzy action-replay before making a decision. That's nonsense. Now if you don't get off the pitch straightaway and let the match continue, I'll abandon it in favour of the Swifts.'

The manager deflated like a pricked balloon. He went away muttering, leaving his players to sort themselves out as best they could.

26

'C'mon, we can still beat this lot even with half a team!' cried the Dynamos' leading scorer, taking over the captaincy.

Getting so steamed up, though, had ruined the quality of their football and the Dynamos never looked likely to break their scoring hoodoo. Against all logic, the Swifts seemed to be holding out for a shock victory, despite the generous amount of added time being allowed for the long dispute.

'Blow that whistle, ref!' pleaded Luke's dad from the touchline. 'This game's going on for ever.'

The referee obliged – but not for the desired reason. In the dying seconds, Tubs made a clumsy challenge for the ball inside the area and the winger collapsed like an imploded factory chimney. Appeals rang out from all around the pitch. The referee took a deep breath, then blew a shrill peep and pointed to the spot.

Penalty!

'The kid dived!' Tubs complained loudly.

'Not fair, ref!' Big Ben joined in. 'You've just given it to make up for all that other business.'

'Don't argue, lads,' the referee said, almost apologetically. 'You won't change my decision.'

He also made it clear that time was up. 'The

game's over apart from the actual penalty kick.
No rebound will be allowed.'

Sanjay and the new captain tried to outstare
each other while the rest of the players stood
around the edge of the area. There was nothing
more anybody else could do. If the penalty went
in, there would have to be a replay. It all
depended on this kick. Or at least they thought
so.

As his opponent ran in to shoot, Sanjay
decided to go to his left. It was a good guess. He
dived and pulled off a fine save, parrying the
well-placed drive. He didn't care where the ball

went. The goalie jumped to his feet just before he was mobbed by his jubilant teammates.

It took a while for the referee's whistle to restore some kind of order. 'Doesn't count!' he announced. 'Goalkeeper moved before the ball was struck. The penalty will have to be retaken.'

The referee suddenly went from villain to hero in the eyes of the Dynamos. They had another chance to save the game, but the Swifts felt crushed by the disappointment. The kicker respotted the ball, turned away from the goal and walked slowly back, planning what he should do.

Luke's commentary was now little more than a whispered croak as he almost choked on the tension of the moment. Most of the players didn't even dare to look.

'So close to glory. Will triumph turn to disaster? Sanjay crouches on his line again, wondering which way to go. Will the kicker try and put it in the same place or not? It's a game of double bluff. Who's going to win this crucial psychological duel?'

Luke's English class at school had recently been studying Rudyard Kipling's famous poem, *If*. His subconscious mention of the poet's two impostors, Triumph and Disaster, triggered off

29

half-remembered snatches of lines in his fertile mind:

*If you can keep your head
When all about you are losing theirs . . .
You'll be a man, my son!*

'Keep your head, Sanjay,' he burbled to himself in the nerve-wracking silence before the kick. 'Be a man, my son!'

The penalty-taker decided to rely on brute strength rather than placement. He blasted the ball with all his might, but Sanjay this time held his position in the centre of the goal. He didn't want to give the referee any excuse to rule out a save.

If Sanjay had dived either way, he'd have missed it. The ball came straight at him like a laser. His block was based on sheer instinct for survival, and it was just as well that his goalie's reflexes were razor sharp. If he hadn't raised his arms in front of his face in time, the cannonball would probably have knocked his head off!

As it was, Sanjay was sent tumbling backwards into the net – but the ball didn't go with him. It went spiralling away somewhere up into the air and the kicker sank to his knees in

despair as the Swifts ran past him to lift their saviour shoulder high. The match was won – and lost.

'You're the man, Sanjay!' Luke cried out. 'The main man.'

Their noisy celebrations continued in the changing room, in stark contrast to the deathly hush on the other side of the thin partition. Luke was the most raucous of the lot, but his dad and uncle at least made an attempt to offer their commiserations to the losers.

They were quite relieved in a sense to find the Dynamos' door closed and locked. 'Best not to disturb them, eh?' whispered Ray.

'Aye, reckon so,' nodded his elder brother. 'Hurry the lads up. We'll slip away before the Dynamos' chappie wants to see that video of yours!'

Luke of course made a special point of watching the tape as soon as he got home – in private on the portable TV set in his bedroom.

'Ah well!' he sighed after he'd reviewed the crossbar incident several times. 'I guess everybody's human. Even referees!'

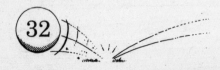

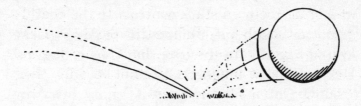

3　Football Fantasy

It was dark too early now for the Swifts to
practise outdoors in midweek. Luke had them
reporting for duty instead on the village recreation ground on Saturday mornings – so long
as there wasn't a school match arranged.

Not that any fixture clash would have
disrupted the Swifts' training plans too much.
Only Sanjay and the Garner twins were regular
members of the Comprehensive's Year 8 soccer
team, but Luke was ever hopeful of being called
up himself to play. He kept those Saturdays free.

After their epic cup victory, however, a team

get-together was a must. They all wanted to savour it further by re-living their many lucky escapes.

'Guess it was just one of those games,' said Titch, shaking his head. 'I bet the Dynamos wouldn't have scored if we'd still been playing now.'

'Better watch out, Skipper. If we go on giant-killing like this in the cup, they'll be calling us Luke's Flukes!' laughed Gary.

'Hey! Got a nice ring to it, that,' his twin grinned. 'I prefer it to Swillsby Swifts. Can we change our name mid-season, Skipper?'

Luke gave him a hard stare. 'No, we can't. Besides, it wasn't fluky. Good teams make their own luck.'

'Well how come we had so much, then?' chortled Tubs. 'We're rubbish!'

'Speak for yourself,' Sanjay cut in, smirking. 'It was you who gave away that last minute penalty, and it was me who saved it – twice!'

'OK, OK, we know,' Tubs conceded. 'But I hardly touched the guy.'

'Can't say I blame him for diving out the way,' Titch said. 'He was probably scared you'd roll on him and squash him flat.'

'I keep thinking about that great bust-up with

34

the ref,' said Brain. 'Did the ball really go in? I couldn't see from where I was.'

'The ref said it wasn't a goal, so it wasn't a goal,' Luke said simply. 'Rule number one of good sportsmanship: the referee is always right.'

'Even when he's wrong, Skip?' chipped in Dazza, their right-winger.

'Well, everybody makes mistakes. All teams receive their fair share of good and bad decisions over a season. You just have to accept them and get on with the game.'

Big Ben looked thoughtful for a moment, which is not easy to do when you're standing in the middle of a draughty changing cabin in your Batman boxer shorts. His long thin legs stuck out of them like a couple of cricket stumps. 'By the way, Luke, what *did* that video show?'

Luke liked to be called Skipper at Swifts' sessions, but he let Big Ben's lapse go uncorrected. He was unnaturally evasive with his response too. 'Oh, nothing worth mentioning,' he said, adding a little nervous cough. 'You know what Ray's filming is like. He's not exactly Steven Spielberg with the camera, is he?'

'So couldn't you tell?'

'Nah, the ball bounced down behind Sanjay and went out of sight.'

35

'I got in the way of all the shots last Sunday,' the goalie grinned.

'Not surprised with a head your size,' Tubs laughed, getting his own back for the many jibes he had to put up with from Sanjay.

'Can we watch the video of the game sometime, Skipper?' asked Brain.

'Er, no, sorry,' Luke apologized. 'It got wiped off by mistake.'

'What! You mean I won't be able to see all my saves again?' gasped Sanjay in genuine dismay. 'How did it happen?'

'Dad went and recorded *The X-Files* over it.'

'Bet even they couldn't solve this mystery!' laughed Gary. 'Was it a goal or wasn't it? Is Sanjay really an alien?'

'It's like that Geoff Hurst goal in the '66 World Cup Final at Wembley,' said Big Ben. 'Y'know, when his shot hit the bar. They're still arguing now about whether or not it bounced down over the line.'

'The linesman said it did, that's all that matters,' Titch pointed out. 'If it wasn't for him, England might not have won the World Cup.'

'Tofik Bakhramov.'

'Pardon, Skip,' said Dazza. 'You say something?'

'Yes, Tofik Bakhramov,' Luke repeated. 'That was the name of the Russian linesman that day.'

The whole cabin burst out laughing at yet another example of Luke's encyclopedic knowledge of the game's trivia. 'You're a mine of useless information,' Gregg teased him. 'I bet you even know the names of all the people in the crowd as well.'

'I know three of them,' Luke smiled. 'Philip Crawford, Ray Crawford and Harold Crawford.'

'Your dad and uncle were actually at that World Cup Final? Magic! Who's this Harold, though?'

'My grandad. He got tickets for the big match and took his kids. They were only about our age at the time. Dad still talks about seeing Hurst's hat-trick.'

That was the cue for most of them to pick up the famous commentary. *'Some people are on the pitch . . . they think it's all over – it is now!'*

Luke wished that he might come out with something equally memorable like that one day himself on TV. He'd just have to keep practising.

'Well it's all over now for the Dynamos, that's for sure,' he grinned. 'But not for us. Up the Swifts! We're gonna win the cup!'

'Dream on, Skipper,' chuckled Tubs. 'Dream on!'

. . . the cross comes over into the penalty area and there's skipper Luke Crawford on the end of it as usual. You just can't keep this boy out of the game. He controls the ball on his chest and as it drops, he smacks it fiercely on the volley with his left foot . . .

. . . the keeper has no chance of reaching it. Ohhh! The ball hits the bar and bounces down and out again. Is it a goal? Yes – no – nobody's sure. Not even the Russian linesman . . .

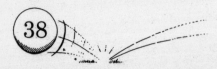

. . . it doesn't matter. Luke has saved the officials from having to make a controversial decision. He's reacted quicker than anybody else and met the rebound with his head, guiding the ball over the stranded keeper into the opposite corner of the net . . .

. . . what a goal! What a player! Already Luke Crawford is well into his famous goal celebration routine. He performs a sequence of acrobatic tumbles, leaps and somersaults that would surely win a gold medal in the Olympic gymnastics competition . . .

. . . that was Luke's second goal of the game, giving his team a four–nil lead. He's made the other two goals as well, but you can bet he'll want to set the seal on this Cup Final by scoring a hat-trick. It'll put his name into the record books yet again . . .

. . . it doesn't take the skipper long. He wins the ball himself inside his own half and sets off on an amazing solo run, demonstrating all his dribbling skills to the cheering crowds. He's beaten one, two, three, four men so far and now the keeper's coming out to try and narrow the shooting angle. Luke has no intention of shooting. He sells the poor keeper a wicked dummy, leaving him sprawled on the grass, nips

past him and runs the ball cheekily into the empty net . . .

. . . he treats his fans to another exhibition of his acrobatics, this time taking the ball with him and juggling it up in the air at the same time. Incredible! Is there nothing this boy can't do? Many people rate him the finest footballer ever, but Luke just shakes his head. 'That honour belongs to Johan,' he always says modestly . . .

. . . and now, at the final whistle, after skippering his side to an overwhelming five–nil victory, Luke is rewarded by meeting his long-time hero. The trophy is presented to him by none other than Johan Cruyff, the legendary Flying Dutchman, the man who inspired Luke to grace the game of football with his tremendous talents . . .

. . . what an emotional scene! The two stars shake hands and embrace in mutual respect before Luke Crawford holds the silver trophy up high to huge roars from the crowd. They think it's all over – it is now. It's a dream come true . . .

'Luke! C'mon, wake up, Luke!' yelled his dad from the bottom of the stairs. 'Match day, sleepy-head. We've got to be off soon. Get up!'

Luke struggled up on to his elbow and

scratched his tousled mop of fair hair. The dream remained so vivid in his mind, he could still picture himself side by side with the great Johan.

'It's got to mean something,' he murmured, lost in wonder. 'Perhaps it's an omen. Perhaps the Swifts really are gonna go all the way . . .'

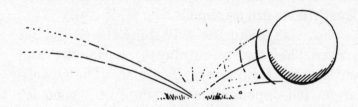

4   Misfits

After the dream came reality – the battle for precious league points.

Luke hated the thought of the Swifts being relegated in their first season. He hadn't formed the team with that possibility in mind at all. He'd set his original sights on promotion.

This was another away game, but much nearer Swillsby. One day, Luke hoped, the Swifts might roll up at some venue with a great cavalcade of cars to impress the home side with the strength of their support. It could even be worth a goal start, as they knew to their own cost.

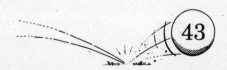

43

As usual, however, they were fortunate to muster three vehicles. Instead of sweeping into the car park in a cloud of dust, they trickled almost apologetically through the gates and bumped across the field towards the changing hut with hardly anyone noticing their arrival. At least they were on time.

That was about the only thing the Swifts got right. They were outplayed, outfought and outclassed from start to finish. Their well-organized opponents were simply too good for them in every department and made the most of their superior abilities.

Sanjay let the first goal in through his legs and conceded the seventh a minute from time. Luke was back 'helping' in defence and deflected a shot that Sanjay had covered straight to the feet of an unmarked attacker.

It wasn't a matter of luck suddenly deserting them. They were lucky only to lose 7–0. It might easily have been twice that many.

'Ah well, it was nice while it lasted,' sighed Big Ben in the hut afterwards, examining a number of bruises on his legs.

'What was?' asked Gary.

'Winning. I might have got used to that, given time.'

44

'Yeah, back to normal now,' said Tubs. 'If there's one thing we're consistently good at, it's getting stuffed!'

The remark was too flippant for Luke. 'Look, we'd do a lot better if only we believed in ourselves more. Then we might surprise a few people by showing them we can play a bit.'

'It'd surprise me for a kick-off,' Tubs grunted. 'I mean, just look at us, all shapes and sizes. A bunch of misfits.'

'Hark at the blubber mountain!' Sanjay cut in.

'OK, so I'm fat,' Tubs snapped back, for once losing his sense of humour. 'Most of us are here 'cos we know nobody else would have us.'

The twins glanced at each other and almost telepathically burst into song together: *'Always look on the bright side of life!'*

'That's half the trouble,' Luke retorted. 'I wish you'd all start to take things more seriously — before it's too late. You just seem to turn up every Sunday to kick a ball about, not caring whether we win or lose.'

'I thought that was the name of the game, Skip,' said Dazza. 'Y'know, enjoying our soccer was more important than the final result.'

'Well, yes it is, but we enjoy it far more when we've won, don't we?'

'Sure,' Gary agreed, 'but no need to get too heavy. We've only lost a footie match. It's not a disaster.'

'Not like the end of the world,' added Gregg.

'I know that,' Luke insisted. 'But it might be the end of the Swifts if we drop out of the League. I mean, the squad might break up. And who'd bother to run another team in the village if I packed it in too?'

'At last some good news,' Sanjay laughed. 'The skipper's thinking of hanging up his boots!'

'Oh well, if that's the way you feel,' Luke said sadly.

'Don't take it personally, Skipper. Only joking.

47

I mean, where would we be without you?'

'Top of the league?' Gary suggested and then took cover as Luke threw a sweaty sock at him.

'Are you saying we don't try?' said Big Ben accusingly. 'Just look at my bruises. I didn't get those sunbathing in the penalty box, you know.'

'I appreciate that,' said Luke, smoothing the centre-back's ruffled feathers. 'But all of us need to practise our skills more and get fitter. And we've got to work together properly as a team to take the pressure off you people in defence for a while.'

The skipper decided to tell the others of his dream, hoping it might inspire them. He wisely left out mention of his own heroic deeds in scoring a hat-trick, but he couldn't resist the part about the cup being presented by the maestro.

His players found it impossible to stifle their giggles. 'You and your Johan,' rumbled Tubs. 'Pity he doesn't know how much you idolize him.'

'You reckon this dream of yours was a sign, then, that we might really win the cup?' said Brain.

'Why not? Somebody's got to, haven't they? Positive thinking!'

'It could be you!' intoned Gary, imitating the

48

Lottery's lucky finger of fate.

'Yeah, but not us,' wheezed Tubs, pulling on his marquee-sized coat. 'C'mon, time to go home. Let's leave Luke to his dreams.'

Luke sighed and consoled himself with Kipling's words:

> *'If you can dream, and not make dreams*
> *your master . . .*
> *You'll be a man, my son!'*

He fully recognized that it would take more than dreams to boost the Swifts' confidence. It would take a lot of hard work – and luck. And finding one or two new players from somewhere to bolster their squad wouldn't do any harm either . . .

A small, under-strength pool of players was a problem that the Swifts shared with Swillsby Comprehensive School.

The Year 8 group in particular was a victim of falling numbers, though this was due more to the sharp tongue of their sports teacher, 'Frosty' Winter, than to any decline in the local birthrate. Several promising players had already dropped out of the soccer squad.

Luke wasn't one of them. His love of the game ensured that he hadn't missed a single school team training session. He always bounced back from Frosty's sarcastic criticisms of his abilities like a ball off a crossbar.

He also attended as many of their matches as possible. Keeping soccer statistics was his hobby and Luke had logged details of every game they'd played since he'd joined the school. Sometimes he had to rely on cousin Jon, Uncle Ray's son, for accounts of away matches, but Jon wasn't that reliable. He was the Comp's star performer and not interested in facts and figures.

If Luke was really desperate for information, he had to ask Frosty and that was even worse. Frosty's memory of who'd scored seemed even shorter than his temper, especially after a Comp defeat – a common occurrence.

The teacher knew, however, that Luke would be on hand if other players failed to show up, even though turning to such an emergency substitute was very much a last resort. The boy's previous catastrophic appearances still tended to wake him up in the middle of the night in a cold sweat.

Frosty feared that he was going to have to risk using Luke once more to make up the numbers

50

for their next match, a home fixture against
Clevefield Comprehensive. Four of the regulars
were needed for county cross-country trials on
the same morning.

Fortunately, his two best players were still
available: Jon Crawford and captain Matthew
Clarke. But Matthew's growing disenchantment
with representing the school only increased
further when he saw the extra names on the
team sheet.

'Not Loony Luke,' he groaned, gazing in disbelief at the sports noticeboard. 'Wish I'd gone in
for the cross-country now.'

Centre-back Adam, a teammate also of Matthew and Jon for their Sunday side, Padley Panthers, was quick to agree. 'There's Big Ben and Tubs too. We've lost before we even start.'

'Yeah, and the only decent player the Sloths *have* got ain't here,' Matthew scowled, using his derogatory nickname for the Swifts. 'Brain is too scared of Frosty to come to any of the practices.'

'Think I might just stay in bed,' grunted Adam.

Frosty anxiously counted heads as the boys arrived on Saturday morning and breathed a sigh of relief when he reached twelve. Until he realized he had included Sanjay's younger brother, still at the primary school.

'Rather pick him than Luke, if I could,' Frosty murmured under his breath, resigned to his fate.

Then Adam strolled casually into the changing room. The defender was ten minutes late, but Frosty welcomed him like the prodigal son. Adam had to duck quickly away. He'd been bracing himself for the expected blast about his timekeeping and lost his cool when he thought for one horrible moment that Frosty was actually going to kiss him!

The teacher struggled to put on a serious face to break the 'bad' news to Luke. 'Sorry, it's the

subs' bench for you again,' he began, tossing him a black and white striped shirt. 'Hope you don't mind.'

It came as no surprise that he'd been lumbered with the number thirteen top as usual – Frosty's pathetic little private joke. Luke pulled it over his head straightaway, not wanting to let him have the satisfaction of seeing his disappointment.

'Funny how he can never find any other spare shirt when I'm involved,' Luke muttered. 'But I'll show him, given half a chance.'

Despite all Frosty's best endeavours, the number thirteen was soon to find himself allowed a far bigger fraction than that . . .

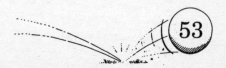

53

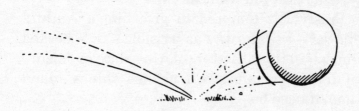

5 Frostbite

Midway through the first half, Tubs pulled up lame.

Frosty whistled the game to a halt and went across to the overweight full-back. With the Comp already 2–0 down, he was not feeling sympathetic. 'The winger's running rings round you. What's the matter?'

Tubs grimaced. 'Think I've done my groin in, sir. Felt a tweak playing for the Swifts last Sunday and now it's got worse.'

Frosty glanced round in panic towards Luke. The substitute was already warming up on the

touchline. 'Can't you carry on? How bad is it?'

'Bad, sir, sorry. It's agony!'

As Tubs hobbled from the field, Frosty reluctantly signalled his sub to come on and Luke was by his side in an instant.

'Where do you want me, sir?'

Frosty felt tempted to give him a truthful answer – as far away as possible – but checked himself in time. 'Better take his place in defence till half-time and we'll change things round then, if need be.'

Luke didn't mind where he played. The main thing was that he was on the pitch. On Sundays he gave himself licence to roam, which meant chasing after the ball wherever it went, and he found it very difficult to curb his natural instincts. He always wanted to be where the action was.

Now he forced himself deliberately to stay back in defence and mark Clevefield's left-winger. He found it a terrific strain, watching from a distance as the Comp attacked down the other side of the pitch. Even to commentate he needed binoculars.

'After the Comp's wretched start, they've now brought on their underrated utility player, Luke Crawford, to shore up the defence. If they can stop

leaking goals, the team have got the quality strikers to get them back into this game. And here's the best of them on the ball as I speak. Luke's multi-talented cousin Jon cuts inside from the wing, creating the space to shoot. Will he hit it with his right or his left? He's lethal with both feet, just like Johan Cruyff . . .'

'Belt up, will you!'

'Eh?' Luke was just getting into full flow when he had to break out of commentary mode to see who'd interrupted him. The winger was glaring at him, but Luke was equally irritated. He hadn't been able to describe Jon's dipping shot

that narrowly cleared the crossbar. 'What's up with you?'

'You! That's what's up. I'm not gonna put up with you droning on like that for the rest of the match – so just shut it, OK?'

'No, it's not OK,' retorted Luke and switched his imaginary microphone back on – full volume. *'The Clevefield winger is obviously rattled now that he knows he's met his match with his new marker. He may not get another kick . . . Owww!'*

The boy made sure he did get another kick – on the back of Luke's legs – before nipping out the way of any possible retaliation. 'That was just a friendly warning,' he sneered. 'If you open your stupid mouth again, I'll put my boot in that instead next time.'

With the ball at the other end of the pitch, nobody had seen the incident and Luke knew there was no point in complaining to the referee. Frosty wouldn't do anything about it. He had to suffer in silence, nursing the blow to his legs and to his pride.

Luke didn't much fancy tangling physically with the tall winger. He comforted himself by imagining a notice of apology at the bottom of the screen. *'We are sorry for the temporary loss of sound. The game will continue in vision only.*

Normal service will be resumed as soon as possible, but in the meantime, here is some music...'

The winger looked round accusingly. There was a loud humming noise coming from somewhere, although he couldn't be quite sure who or what was making it. But he had a pretty good idea.

By the interval, the Comp were trailing 4–0 and wishing it was full time instead. It might have been even worse. Just before the whistle, Luke had saved a fifth by blocking the ball on the goalline, allowing Sanjay to recover and dive on top of it.

'Good stop, that, Luke,' said Jon as the players trudged towards Frosty for the expected ear-bashing. 'You couldn't have been better positioned.'

Luke grinned, basking in any praise he received. It was so rare, the novelty never wore off. 'Don't suppose old Frosty will mention it.'

'Unusual style, though,' his cousin smiled, amused by the way the ball had rolled against Luke's neck. 'What were you doing lying there like that in the first place?'

'Got tripped up in the goalmouth scramble, didn't I? Probably that winger. Real head-case, he is.'

'You mean the one who's scored a hat-trick?'

Luke ignored the implied jibe at his defensive deficiencies. 'Yeah, that's the one. He keeps having a go at me. Dead vicious, like.'

Luke explained quickly what had been happening and while Jon took it seriously enough, Matthew clearly didn't. Luke could see him smirking when Jon had a quiet word with the captain about it. Adam was sniggering too, not really listening to all Frosty's criticisms.

'This is just a damage limitation exercise now,' the teacher told them. 'We've already lost this match, but we need to stop it becoming a rout.

That winger's murdering us.'

'He's certainly committing GBH on me,' Luke muttered grimly.

Frosty made wholesale positional changes for the second half, directing Adam to mark the winger. Luke was moved up on to the wing himself with instructions to hug the touchline. Out of harm's way, Frosty hoped.

Adam intended to make an immediate impact. Straight after the restart he wandered over to introduce himself to their first-half tormentor, holding out his hand. 'Congratulations!' he said with a grin.

'What d'yer mean?' the winger said, eyeing him suspiciously. They'd already clashed a couple of times in the penalty area, fouls that the referee had chosen to overlook.

'I gather you managed to shut our idiot number thirteen up. Well done, we've been trying to do that ourselves all season. How did you do it?'

The boy relaxed his guard slightly and accepted Adam's handshake. 'Well, I just . . .'

He stopped as he became aware of the pain in his right hand. Adam had also gripped his arm and now tightened the pressure. 'Hey! You're hurting me,' he complained.

'Yeah, I know,' Adam snarled. 'If the teacher says mark somebody, I mark 'em all right. I think three goals are enough, don't you, pal?'

The winger nodded his head furiously. 'OK, OK, I get the message,' he cried. 'I'll back off.'

Adam released him as a few spectators began to show an interest in their little tête-à-tête. 'Good man, I knew you'd see my point of view. Enjoy the second half.'

That was the closest the winger got to Adam for the rest of the match. He didn't even risk shaking hands with him again after the final whistle.

With their hat-trick hero mysteriously subdued, the Clevefield attack carried little more threat. Swillsby were able to go on the offensive themselves and would have scored sooner than they did if Luke hadn't kept popping up in the unlikeliest of places. His untimely involvement disrupted all their most promising moves.

'Keep out on that wing!' Frosty growled at him. 'You're a menace. I should have given you one of their red shirts, not one of ours!'

The teacher's stinging words were like water off an ugly duckling's back to Luke. He was used to them. He was running free and enjoying himself again, unshackled by any defensive duties.

'The Comp are well on top now, despite the scoreline,' his resurrected commentary burbled happily. *'There's only one team in it this half with Luke Crawford breathing fresh life into their attack. It's only a matter of time before the goals must come. And look, here's the captain now, linking up with Jon outside the area before letting fly at goal . . . Ow! . . . Oh dear, the shot's been blocked . . . pity!'*

It was more than a pity for Matthew. Luke had failed to mention that it was the player-commen-

tator himself who had inadvertently wandered across the line of the captain's drive that was destined for the net.

Matthew's language made the Dynamos' foul-mouthed captain seem like he had a limited vocabulary. Threats and curses rained down on Luke and he took these far more seriously than Frosty's rantings. He retired to the wing and busied himself there with his commentary. He described in lavish detail not only the two goals Matthew and Jon did eventually score, but also Big Ben's comical own goal, back-heading the ball past Sanjay.

'Well, five-two, could have been worse,' Luke babbled to Jon as they trooped in to the changing rooms. 'Great goal of yours. Johan would have been proud of that one.'

His cousin gave his habitual, casual shrug, a characteristic mannerism that he'd made almost into an art form. 'Yeah, not bad, I suppose. Soz about Matt. He was out of order there, swearing at you like that.'

Luke tried to copy the shrug, but didn't quite pull it off. He mistimed his shoulders, making it look like he had a nervous tic. 'No sweat. I've got more important things to worry about than Matthew.'

64

'Such as?'

'Such as the injury to Tubs. Looks like he could be out of action for a while. He might have to miss our next cup match.'

'Shame. You might have a fair chance of getting through as well.'

Luke looked at him. 'How d'yer mean? We don't even know who we're playing yet.'

Jon grinned. 'Hasn't Dad told you? He got the news yesterday.'

Luke couldn't believe it. Uncle Ray was the Swifts' official team contact and received all the letters from the League Secretary before passing them to him. 'You're having me on.'

'No, straight up. You've been drawn at home – against Brenton Blues. Aren't they in the same division as you?'

Luke leapt up and punched the air in delight. 'Ye–es!' he cried out. 'We can lick them OK. Quarter-finals here we come!'

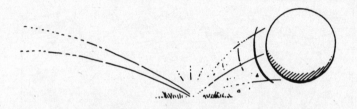

6   Tactical Changes

Sitting at the desk in his bedroom, Luke faithfully recorded the details of the school match into his notebook. This time he used red ink rather than the usual black. Personal appearances always deserved to stand out. He made special mention of his vital role in both defence and attack.

He then switched on the computer to prepare for the Swifts' home league game the following afternoon. In the wake of Tubs's injury, the innovative coach wanted to devise a different team formation with adventurous, new tactics.

Instructions and diagrams filled several pages on the screen and churned out of the printer on to the floor.

Luke was in his element. Immersed in his own planning, with the radio blaring out a live match commentary and the latest football scores, he didn't even hear the calls to go down for his tea. Some things were more important than food.

He was up early next day, delivering the print-outs to his team members around the village so they'd have a chance to digest their contents before the game. He didn't bother calling on

Brain. Their star winger was severely dyslexic. Brain could read a pass far better than any words.

A quarter of an hour before kick-off, his team-mates were still poring over the pages in the changing cabin when Brain arrived late. 'Hello, what's all that?' he asked.

'Skip's latest world-beating schemes,' Dazza grinned. 'Haven't you got yours yet?'

Brain shook his head. 'He knows it'd be a waste of time giving them to me.'

'Lucky you!' laughed Gary.

'Lucky you, you mean, Gary,' said Luke. 'You're one of my new wing-backs. Just think of all that great attacking you'll be able to do up the left side!'

'Yeah, and all that slogging back again when some idiot goes and loses the ball,' he replied, deliberately catching Luke's eye.

'That's worrying me a bit too, Skip,' Dazza admitted. 'If you're expecting me to keep running back to help in defence, I'll be too knackered to do any real attacking.'

Luke brushed aside his misgivings. 'Rubbish! You'll love it, always being involved in the game. A lot of teams are using this system now – a three-man defence, with wing-backs to support

69

the midfield and attack.'

'You didn't dream all this guff up then?' said Big Ben, chucking his papers on to the floor.

Luke gathered them up and collected everyone else's too so they wouldn't deliberately lose them. He'd dish them out again for discussion at the next practice. 'Of course I didn't dream it,' he defended himself. 'When I played for the Comp yesterday at full-back and on the wing, I saw how easily you could combine the two positions.'

Tubs was leaning against the cabin wall. 'Glad I'm just watching today. Running's not for me. I can barely even walk at the moment.'

'Nobody would notice any difference,' Sanjay joked.

The grin was soon wiped off the goalkeeper's face. The ambitious changes proved disastrous, the players unable to cope with the demands of the system. Far from having just three men at the back, they could have done with about a dozen. Sanjay lost count of the number of times he picked the ball out the back of the net. In the end, he didn't even like to ask what the score was.

The Swifts sat around on the benches for a while afterwards, shell-shocked and exhausted, lacking the energy to start getting dressed.

'Back to the drawing-board, I reckon, Skipper,' said Brain.

Luke let out a loud sigh. 'Bound to be a few teething problems at first. Nothing we can't sort out in training. The tactics just need a bit of fine tuning, that's all.'

'Fine tuning!' Big Ben scoffed. 'They need a sledgehammer taken to them, if you ask me, and then thrown on the dump!'

'I reckon that mongrel had the best idea what to do with those print-outs,' observed Tubs, smirking. 'I think it's called passing an opinion!'

They burst out laughing, recalling the hilarious half-time incident. It would take some forgetting. Luke was in the middle of his team-talk, desperately attempting to salvage something from the wreckage, when a stray dog wandered up to their base-camp. It sniffed around their chewed slices of orange, then cocked its leg and piddled all over the pile of papers.

The look on the skipper's face was classic. For once, he'd been totally at a loss for words, his mouth still working, but with no sound coming out. As the Swifts fell about, the opposition had gazed across from their own camp in puzzlement. They couldn't fathom how a team that was

losing so heavily seemed to be having so much fun.

Swillsby Swifts had two more league matches to play before the third-round tie, the second of which was away to their cup opponents, Brenton Blues.

Luke was determined to persevere with his new strategies, sure that they would help to bring the best out of the players – eventually. 'If at first you don't succeed . . .' he murmured, wondering whether that was part of Kipling's poem as well. He couldn't quite remember. He knew he'd heard it somewhere before.

He was in front of the computer again, revising the plans before reprinting them. Nobody fancied having the original papers back.

'I shouldn't have tried to rush things through like that,' Luke mused, admitting – at least to himself – that he might have made a mistake. 'They couldn't take it all in at once.'

He broke off to study a tape of England's 4–1 thrashing of the Dutch at Wembley during Euro '96. It was Luke's favourite viewing. He'd watched it over and over again, analysing and admiring England's style of play. If Cruyff was Luke's footballing hero, then Terry Venables,

73

the England coach at the time, was his tactical genius.

'It's all about having the right players for the right jobs,' Luke said aloud to himself, returning to tinker with his formation further on the computer. 'Trouble is, I've got the right jobs, but the wrong players.'

Christmas was fast approaching and unless he could sign any new faces before the League's end-of-year transfer deadline, Luke knew that he'd have to make do with what he'd already got. He knuckled down to his task and at the Swifts' next training session, he presented everybody, including Brain, with a fresh batch of print-outs.

'You're serious about this, aren't you?' said Big Ben, leafing through them wearily. 'You're not going to give up.'

'Dead right!' Luke beamed. 'What's good enough for England is good enough for us.'

'I should point out,' said Mark, Big Ben's usual partner in the centre of defence, 'that international players are a little better than us.'

'C'mon, let's humour him,' sighed Big Ben. 'We'll give it another go.'

To their credit, the Swifts worked as hard as Luke could remember, but there was a limit to what they could achieve in practice. The true

test of their progress would be provided by the opposition on Sunday.

When that day came, a generous examiner might have given the Swifts six out of ten for effort. They did manage to match the England score, albeit in reverse, but there the similarity ended.

Luke and Brain – in theory – played behind Gregg as the main striker, but wing-backs Gary and Dazza were too often caught out of position. Luke couldn't really complain. After all, he only found himself where he should be by accident. Carried away by the excitement of the game, the skipper scoured the pitch, as always, rarely to be seen very far from the ball.

'Oh well, not too bad, I guess,' he reflected ruefully, bringing his Swifts' record book up to date later. 'Only lost four-one this time.'

At least his team had proved to themselves that the system might be made to work. They'd created more chances than usual and Dazza's strike near the end, sprinting on to Gary's cross to lash home a beauty, rewarded the Swifts with more than a mere consolation goal. It offered hope!

The next two games, in both league and cup, were now against the Blues and Luke kept

75

repeating his main message to the players in training. 'If we can't outplay 'em, we'll outnumber 'em,' he stressed, quoting Venables's guiding motto. 'We must try and get more of our men around the ball than theirs, especially in midfield.'

'We need extra help at the back as well, though,' Mark said. 'We can't afford to get overrun there like we were in the last match at times.'

'Point taken,' Luke conceded, 'but if we can win more of the ball in midfield, they won't be able to put our goal under pressure so much. Attack is the best form of defence!'

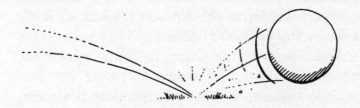

7   Christmas Tree

Brenton Blues were yo-yoing up and down in mid-table week by week, their inconsistency making them as likely to lose as to win games. It was also sufficient to give Luke genuine cause for optimism.

'With a bit of luck, we might just catch them on an off day,' he said brightly on the way to Brenton.

'Huh! With a lot of luck, more like,' grunted Sanjay.

'With a *lot* of luck, they might even have two off days,' Titch grinned. 'Today and in the cup next Sunday!'

'It's crucial we play well today, anyway,' Luke stressed. 'We need the points more than they do, and a result here would give us the psychological edge for the cup-tie at home.'

Sanjay looked at his skipper almost pityingly. 'You don't half talk some rubbish,' he began, then corrected himself. 'No, sorry, you don't *half* talk it – you do it all the time!'

'And the amazing thing is,' Tubs joined in between guffaws, 'he makes it sound like he actually believes we're good enough to beat this lot.'

Luke glanced at his dad, but knew that he had to stick up for himself. 'We *are!*' he insisted gamely. 'And we'll be even better when you're fit to play again, Tubs. You've left a big hole in our team.'

Tubs wondered for a moment if Luke was trying to be funny, but he might have guessed that Sanjay would spot the chance. 'I think you mean a crater, don't you, Skipper?' the goalkeeper giggled.

If this league encounter was going to give any psychological advantage to either team, it was the Swifts that took the initiative. And it was their much abused player-manager who had the honour of putting them ahead.

Brain set up the goal. He could have netted it himself, dribbling clear into the penalty area, but he saw his skipper unmarked and unselfishly squared the ball across the goal-mouth. It was easier to score than miss, but Luke nearly performed the more difficult option.

Unfortunately, the pass rolled to Luke's left foot. Its main job in life was to save him from hopping along all the time, but now he had to put it to more glamorous use. He shaped to steer the ball over the line but lost his balance and began to topple backwards. The ball skidded from the top of his boot and dollied up into the net off the inside of the post.

Luke lay flat on his back, soaking up the rare moment of perfect bliss. He was so relieved, he almost forgot to do his much-rehearsed, choreographed goal celebration. Suddenly he leapt to his feet and went jigging about the area in a dance that resembled a hyperactive monkey at a rave party. His teammates kept a respectful, embarrassed distance, hoping other people wouldn't think they were with him.

'Ought to be locked up, that kid,' grumbled one of the older home supporters. 'He's off his rocker!'

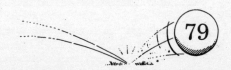

Even Uncle Ray stopped filming. He didn't think it was something that ought to be shown to young children.

Luke soon sobered up. The Blues hit back within a minute, capitalizing on slack marking in the middle of the Swifts' defence. The back three stared at one another accusingly, preferring that to excusing their lapse either to the skipper or, even worse, to an unimpressed Sanjay.

'Can't be helped, we all make mistakes,' Luke reassured his defenders at half-time, hoping nobody would point out that he normally made more than most. He was just thankful he hadn't messed up the open goal. 'We're still level, and there's everything to play for in the second half.'

'Not if we go and gift them any more early Christmas presents like that equalizer,' grumbled Sanjay. 'We're lucky they haven't scored more already. I haven't got enough cover in front of me.'

Under pressure from others, too, Luke agreed to revert to a four-man defence. Gary was deployed to stay tight on the Blues' right-winger whose lively runs had caused them major problems in the first period. It seemed to do the trick. Gary did a good man-marking job on him,

81

keeping the winger much quieter for the rest of the game, and the Swifts succeeded in clinging on for a 1–1 draw.

Their survival was not without its scares, especially when Sanjay fumbled a shot near the end that bobbled out of his hands and rolled just wide of a post, but it was well deserved. At least the Swifts thought so. They changed after the match in high spirits.

'They're no great shakes, these Blues,' said Gregg, voicing the general opinion. 'I reckon we can take them all right next week.'

It was music to Luke's ears. His own confidence seemed to be rubbing off on some of his team and they were beginning to have more faith in their abilities. He felt it was the right moment to unveil his latest plans.

'Our formation needs to be more flexible in future,' he told them. 'We've proved today we can adjust things even during a game, depending on how the other team play. I think it's time to put up the *Christmas tree!*'

'Now I know he's finally cracked,' groaned Sanjay. 'He's gonna block up our goal with a Christmas tree.'

'Yeah, and put Tubs on top as the fairy!' hooted Gary.

Luke joined in the laughter. 'It's just the name of the system 'cos of its shape,' he explained. 'Terry Venables first came up with it. It's a 4–3–2–1 line-up, tapering something like a Christmas tree.'

'How does that help?' asked Brain.

'Well, it makes sure we've got good numbers in defence and midfield when we need them,' Luke enthused. 'And it also gives us a launch-pad for our own attacks.'

'Just listen to him,' smiled Titch. 'He's off again!'

Luke spent part of the week trying to drum up more local support for the Swifts' big cup-tie on the recreation ground. He printed a dozen notices, using computer graphics, and put them on trees and walls around the village. He also pinned a few up in the school corridors.

The ones at the Comp were torn down as soon as Luke turned his back. Matthew even snatched a poster out of his hand and ripped it to pieces in front of him. 'That's what I think of the Sloths,' he snarled, choosing to ignore the fact that his own Panthers had suffered a shock, first-round knock-out by the Swifts. 'Just rubbish to chuck in the bin.'

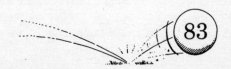

Luke's efforts, however, had not been wasted. Quite a number of people began to gather on the touchline before the kick-off, even if over half of them, he realized, were Blues' supporters. He was delighted to see some parents and schoolmates who had never previously turned up to watch.

'Attracted a crowd,' Gary observed from the changing-room door. 'I hope they haven't all come just to laugh at us.'

'Yeah, it wasn't so bad getting thrashed in private,' said Tubs, 'but I don't fancy being humiliated in public!'

Luke used the spectators as extra motivation for his team before they left the cabin. 'C'mon, men. We don't want to let our fans down. Let's show them how the Swifts can really play.'

'*Fans*, he calls them! He'll be wanting to start up a Swifts' fan club next!' chuckled Tubs, fit enough now to be named as their one and only sub. He was trying not to let it show how keen he was to play and sneaked a quiet word with Luke. 'You'll make sure I come on, won't you, Skipper? Half-time, maybe?'

'Can't promise, Tubs,' he replied. 'But I won't forget you, don't worry. Nice to have you back. We've missed you.'

'No kidding?' He grinned inanely at the flattery.

'Sure. We've had no-one to roll out the bumps on the pitch!'

Luke had to duck out the way of Tubs's playful swipe and then prepared to address his team. Sanjay beat him to it. 'Right, men. All ready?' the goalkeeper cried out.

'I say that!' Luke demanded above the laughter and then grinned. 'OK, c'mon, then. Let's get out there and light up that Christmas tree!'

It was a strange sort of game. It had to be strange when the Swifts had possession of the

ball more than their opponents. That phenomenon had never happened before. The new-look formation, worked on only in Saturday's practice session, denied Brenton space to play their football. The Blues' attacks were crowded out and once they'd broken down, the visitors often didn't find it easy to get the ball back again.

Luke was 'over the moon', as his commentary-jargon would no doubt say. There was no escaping his pitch-wide coverage. It was picked up on all wavelengths as he chased about like an over-excited puppy.

'Swifts are really turning on the style today! They're not letting the Blues settle on the ball and keep putting together slick passing moves of their own. Here's another one now as Dazza eats up the ground down the right, taking the ball out wide to stretch the Blues' shaky back-line yet again. Gregg, Brain and skipper Luke Crawford are waiting in the middle for the cross and over it comes . . . GOOOAAALLL!!!'

It wasn't exactly 'Goal of the Season', but it gave the Swifts a morale-boosting, half-time lead just the same. Gregg mistimed his header, Luke swung at the loose ball and missed, accidentally selling a dummy to two defenders, and

there was Brain lurking behind him to tuck it coolly into the net.

The Blues woke up to the dangers of defeat after the interval and pressed hard, but the Swifts' four-man defence looked more secure. To say the Christmas tree held its shape would be an exaggeration, but at least it stayed upright and didn't collapse.

The equalizer came as a bitter blow. It was stabbed home during a frantic goalmouth scramble, and for a while the visitors gained the upper hand, striving for the winner. Luke brought on Tubs as a panic measure to reinforce their midfield barrier, but it turned out to be an unintentional masterstroke.

With the tie heading towards another 1–1 stalemate and a replay back at Brenton, Tubs latched on to a clearance from Gary. He was a long way out from goal, too far to attempt going on a run – or waddle in his case – so he wound himself up and walloped the ball instead.

It was hit and hope. It was pain and ecstasy. The pain came from an immediate pull in the groin. The ecstasy came from seeing the ball thunder past the keeper's despairing dive as Tubs crumpled to the ground.

88

The hero had to be carried off the pitch by Luke's dad and uncle, which left the ten-man Christmas tree, shorn of its thickest branch, to withstand a raging storm. Somehow it did. The final whistle never sounded so sweet.

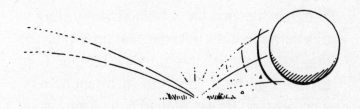

8   Foreign Signing

In his darkened bedroom that evening, Luke basked in the reflected glory of the computer screen's green light. He was drafting his regular match report for the sports page of Uncle Ray's monthly newspaper, the *Swillsby Chronicle*. No creative task gave him more pleasure, fuelling his ambitions one day to be a top soccer reporter. He gazed dreamily at his bold headline and then let the words flow from the keyboard.

CUP GIANT-KILLERS

by our soccer correspondent

Swillsby Swifts 2 – 1 Brenton Blues

The Swifts march on! A magnificent victory in this third round tie puts the soaring Swifts into the last eight of the Sunday League Cup. Cheered on by a large crowd of supporters, who sensed that yet another cup upset was on the cards, Swillsby played with an adventurous, attacking spirit that rocked the visitors. This was the second successive meeting between the two sides, but coach Luke Crawford had modified the Swifts' tactical system since their 1–1 draw in the league. Their new 'Christmas Tree' formation was designed to ensure there would be no gift goals for the Blues. 'Our best performance of the season so far,' said Luke later. 'The boys really played as a team.'

Brian 'Brain' Draper had put the Swifts ahead

by half-time, but when the Blues equalized the game seemed doomed for a replay. Player-manager Luke, however, still had one ace up his sleeve. He brought supersub Anthony 'Tubs' Tompson off the bench to produce the killer punch. Returning from injury, Tubs was hurt again as he blasted the ball home for the winning goal. 'It was worth the pain,' the scorer grinned afterwards. 'I just hope I'm fit for the quarter-finals.'

Skipper Luke is looking even beyond that. 'With a bit of luck,' he said, 'we're hoping this cup run leads all the way to the Final. This could be our year!'

When the *Chronicle* appeared the following week, just before the end of term, Tubs flourished a copy under Luke's nose. 'You've made me sound like a moron,' he protested. 'I didn't say nothing of the sort.'

'You might have done,' said Luke. 'It's called journalistic licence. It lets you put things in your report that maybe aren't strictly accurate. Don't you want to play in the next round, then?'

'Of course I do.'

'Well, then, what's all the fuss about? You got your name in the paper, didn't you?'

'Yeah, and that's another thing,' Tubs said, pulling a face. 'You spelt it all wrong. It's Antony without the "h" and Thompson with one!'

'Soz, I only know you as Tubs,' Luke grinned. 'Anyway, you've got plenty of time to get fit. The quarter-final game is our first one of the New Year, so go easy on the mince pies at Christmas.'

'Cut down on my food!' exclaimed Tubs. 'No fear! I'd rather be fat than fit!'

The Christmas holidays passed far too slowly for Luke.

With no real soccer action, apart from a few kickabouts with Jon in the back garden or with their mates on the recky, he felt at a loose end most of the time. He'd read all his new football annuals by Boxing Day.

Things only returned to normal when he had his Swifts report back for training on the Friday morning after New Year's Day. Luke was so excited about Sunday's big match, he was finding it hard to get to sleep. And he could barely wait to see the players' faces when he revealed his last-minute new signing!

They were going to need as much extra help as possible. Their quarter-final opponents were as tough as they come. The Swifts had been drawn away to Ridgeway Rovers, one of the top first division sides. Luke had wanted to have a good work out with the team and put them through their paces, but his plans were already in jeopardy.

He'd fully expected that the Christmas tree was bound to need a bit of sprucing up after the holidays, but he hadn't anticipated that two vital parts of it would have dropped off. The Garner twins were missing.

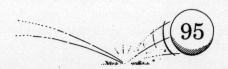

95

'Where are Gary and Gregg?' asked Titch, checking around the cabin as the squad changed into tracksuits. The weather was bitterly cold.

Luke frowned. 'They went up to Scotland to celebrate the New Year with relatives. They're not due back till tomorrow evening.'

'Cutting it a bit fine, isn't it?'

'It's about as welcome as your next-door neighbour learning to play the bagpipes,' Luke muttered. 'Nothing I can do about it, though. Their dad promised they'd be home in time for the game.'

'So long as they don't get snowed in up there,' Mark put in. 'It'd be goodbye cup dreams, if they weren't here.'

'Have you got any more dreams to tell us about, Skipper?' grinned Sean. He was the left-side, middle branch of their Christmas tree, the one with most of the fancy decorations on it. His be-ringed fingers were polishing his boots now to bring up the shine.

Luke shook his head. 'Haven't even had *that* one again since.'

'What about New Year resolutions, then?' Sanjay smiled. 'Made any of them? Like not inventing new tactics every week, for instance.'

'Yeah, and writing no more match reports,'

Tubs suggested.

'Actually, I have made one,' Luke said, cheering up. 'And it concerns all of us.'

'Thought it would do,' Big Ben groaned. 'C'mon, let's hear it.'

'Yeah, the sooner we know what it is, the sooner we can break it,' laughed Tubs. 'Mine didn't last five minutes.'

'What was it?'

'Resolved to lose weight by not eating chocolate. And then I just had to have a caramel bar to console myself! Soz, Skipper!'

'We'll have to get the cabin door widened for you,' Luke said pointedly. 'Anyway, do you want me to tell you or not?'

'Anything to stay in here a bit longer,' said Sanjay to murmurs of agreement. The cabin was draughty, but it was better than being outside. For once, they were happy to let Luke talk as much as he liked.

'Your skipper has firmly resolved that the Swifts will do the Double!' he proclaimed. 'Win the cup and also escape relegation!'

The wooden cabin almost collapsed with the roars of laughter and stamping of boots on bare boards. Luke waited for the rumpus to die down.

'I'm deadly serious, team. And I know just the

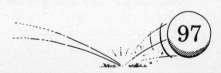

97

guy who's gonna help us do it. My cousin!'

'Jon!' Mark gasped. 'Have you gone and signed Jon up for the Swifts?'

'He's cup-tied,' said Big Ben. 'Played for the Panthers, remember.'

Luke's grin was as wide as the Cheshire cat's. 'No, this isn't Jon. He's a cousin of ours who only arrived in this country over Christmas. The Swifts now boast the League's first Italian import!'

The Swifts were all agog to see their new player. Luke banged twice on the partition wall as a signal and through the adjoining door from the visitors' changing room appeared a tall, athletic-looking figure.

'This is Ricki,' Luke announced. 'Ricki, meet your new teammates.'

Tubs's jaw dropped. 'You're not another Crawford, are you?'

Ricki smiled and shook his head. 'You have plenty Crawfords already,' he said with a strong accent. 'My full name is Ricardo Fortuna.'

'My aunt married an Italian,' Luke explained. 'They've come to live in England for a while so I snapped him up. Just got the registration forms completed before the transfer deadline.'

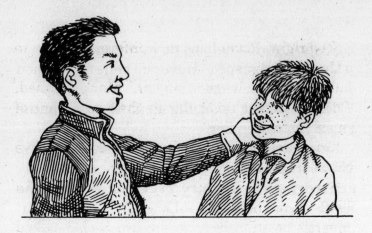

'Fantastic!' said Sanjay with genuine enthusiasm. 'Are you gonna play for the Comp too?'

Ricki looked puzzled and Luke answered for him. 'Ricki's going to Padley High School, I'm afraid. Old Frosty won't be able to get his hands on him, but he'll be playing for us as often as he can.'

'Not every week?' said Brain, disappointed.

'I am sorry,' said Ricki. 'We love rugby in our family too. Rugby is plenty big sport in Italy now.'

'So when he's not playing rugby, he'll turn out for us,' said Luke. 'Starting with the cup match on Sunday!'

'With a name like Fortuna, he's got to bring us good luck,' laughed Dazza. 'And we're sure gonna need loadsa luck against Rovers.'

'Too right. Rovers are in a different league to us,' said Titch.

'Yeah, three leagues higher,' Mark grinned. 'Perhaps we should challenge them to a game of rugby instead.'

'Good idea!' said Tubs. 'I'm better at rugby. I've got the right build for that.'

Sanjay smirked at him. 'You're the size of a whole scrum on your own.'

'What position do you play in, Ricki?' asked Sean.

'In the centre. But I like to score tries too.'

'Luke just tries to score,' Tubs chuckled, wondering if Ricki knew what he was letting himself in for. 'Has he shown you the league table?'

'I've told him we're in a false position,' Luke said quickly. 'With Ricki in the team, things can only get better. He's incredibly fit from doing all his sport in Italy.'

If Ricki was not yet aware of the Swifts' standard of football, the lack of knowledge was mutual. One thing Luke didn't care to admit to his team was that he hadn't even seen his Italian cousin play.

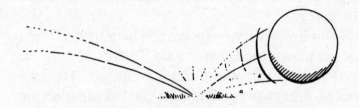

9 Happy New Year?

The Swifts were still talking about Ricki as they drove to the match. His performance at Friday's practice had been patchy – part Jon, part Luke.

'I don't like to say this, but I'm not too sure he's really up to much,' said Mark. 'Seemed to think he was playing rugby half the time, the way he kept catching the ball.'

'Perhaps it was too cold for him,' said Big Ben. 'He's not used to our winter weather yet.'

'Well, let's hope he'll feel more at home playing Rovers,' Mark sighed. 'They're red-hot favourites to win the cup.'

Luke was pleased with the size of the convoy heading for Ridgeway Park in Padley. Five cars trailed behind his dad's, but how he wished there'd been another. Mr Garner had failed to show up at the usual meeting point and the Garner house was empty when they went there to check.

'You know we've only got ten men now, if Ricki doesn't turn up as well,' said Tubs.

'I can count,' Luke said, irritated. 'He'll be there, don't worry. Him and his dad are meeting us at the park. They live right next to it.'

To Luke's undisguised relief, Ricki was already waiting for them near the changing pavilion. He had a rugby ball tucked under his arm.

'What have you got that for?' Luke asked. 'It's football today.'

Ricki grinned. 'Dad always gives me plenty practice with kicking.'

'Just remember, Ricki,' Tubs began, miming the shape of a round ball. 'In soccer, we try and kick the ball under the crossbar, not over it!'

Ricki laughed. 'I like you, Tubs. You make plenty good jokes, yes? We all good jokers here.'

'Yeah, that's right, Ricki, you catch on quick,' he replied. 'The Swifts are plenty big joke!'

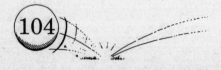

104

There was still no sign of Gary and Gregg by kick-off time and Luke desperately rearranged his line-up to cover for their absence. He didn't even attempt to explain to Ricki about their Christmas tree.

'Just put yourself about plenty,' he instructed his cousin, picking up Ricki's favourite word as well. 'Up and down the pitch, all over, winning the ball. Prove how fit you are. *Comprendo*? Got it?'

'Got it!' he said with a grin, sticking his thumb up. 'No worries.'

Sadly, Luke soon had many things to worry about. Rovers scorched into a 2–0 lead without

even breaking sweat. The first goal came by courtesy of Sean's careless back-pass, finding a Rovers' attacker instead of Sanjay, and the second was a penalty.

Ricki's flying tackle had the desired effect of making the opponent lose control of the ball, but his chosen method wasn't to be found in any soccer coaching manual. He'd dived full-length and wrapped his arms around the boy's ankles to bring him crashing down.

'I am plenty sorry, Skipper,' he said sheepishly after the referee had booked him for the foul. 'I forget.'

Luke sighed. 'Just don't do it again, OK? You were lucky you didn't get yourself sent off.'

The Swifts' supporters on the touchline shuffled their feet. 'I have a terrible feeling this might get very embarrassing,' muttered Luke's dad.

'Didn't help when our brother-in-law applauded Ricki's tackle,' said Ray. 'He'll be wanting him to dive over the line for a try next!'

Jon was with them. The Panthers had no match arranged and he'd come along to cheer his cousins on. 'Ricki's bound to be nervous at first,' he said charitably. 'You wait until he settles down. I reckon he can play a bit. He looked good taking shots at Sanjay in the warm-up.'

'Anybody can look good shooting at Sanjay!' his dad chuckled. 'We want to see him troubling the keeper at the other end.'

As they spoke, a defender wandered idly up to Tubs who was playing in Gregg's role as lone striker at the top of the tree. 'This is gonna be a massacre. How did you lot manage to get as far as these quarter-finals?'

Tubs shrugged his bulky shoulders. 'I think it's called being fluky.'

'Well I reckon your luck's finally run out,' the boy sniggered.

107

'Don't count on it,' smiled Tubs as they both heard Luke coming towards them. 'Our captain probably thinks Johan Cruyff will suddenly come on as sub to rescue us!'

Luke's rambling commentary did seem to be clutching at straws. *The Swifts are not giving up hope yet. Player-manager Luke Crawford's boys are made of sterner stuff nowadays and don't expect to lose games like they used to. They know it only takes one kick to score a goal, and that would put them right back in it. And the Garner twins may yet arrive . . .'*

He broke off. He could scarcely believe his eyes. For a moment, he thought Jon had nipped on to the pitch and gone swooping down the wing with the ball, but then he realized it was cousin Ricki instead. Luke hared off in pursuit, as did Tubs more slowly, but Ricki clearly needed no support.

For a tall lad, he had lightning feet and his body swerves at speed left two baffled Rovers trailing in his wake. As the goalie advanced, Ricki unleashed a rasping shot in his stride from outside the box. The ball curled and dipped and struck the crossbar with a crack that might have echoed over to Italy and back.

'Magic!' cried Dazza. 'That's showed 'em we

mean business.'

'Keep tighter on that big kid,' shouted the Rovers' captain. 'We can't give him room to run at us like that again. He's deadly!'

Ricki's blast out of the blue set the game alight, firing up his own team's flagging spirits and earning the Swifts new respect from their opponents. In one flash of inspiration, he had achieved more than Luke could ever dream of doing. The skipper had to be content with his decision to take the risk of signing his cousin up into Swifts' colours before it was too late.

'That might be the turning point of the Swifts' season,' he told his imagined host of listeners as well as any players nearby. *'Whatever happens in this match, the future looks brighter. The Christmas tree now has a real glittering star!'*

The cup-tie became a more even contest for a time as the Swifts fought fiercely for control of the midfield and enjoyed their fair share of the ball. Rovers were made to work much harder than they'd anticipated, struggling to find a path through the tree's maze of tangled branches. When they finally did so, their third goal brought the first division side very welcome extra breathing space at the interval.

'This is more like it,' Luke praised his team as

they huddled together, quite pleased with themselves, despite the 3–0 scoreline. 'We've not lost yet. Keep it up. All we need is . . .'

Jon came running up to interrupt. 'The Garners are here. Look!'

'Think I must have a bang on the head,' said Ricki, shaking it. 'I am seeing double!'

'It's OK, Ricki,' laughed Sean. 'It's only the twins.'

'Happy New Year, guys,' Tubs welcomed them as they raced from the car to join the group. ''Fraid the party's nearly over, though.'

'Soz, Skipper,' gasped Gregg. 'Car broke down. Had all sorts of problems getting home.'

'Got trouble here too, I gather,' said Gary.

'Not as bad as we thought at first, thanks to Ricki,' grinned Dazza.

'Who?' they chorused.

'It's a long story,' said Luke. 'Just go and get your gear on quick, both of you – at the double!'

The Swifts' Little and Large pairing of Titch and Tubs were the unlucky ones to make way, and Ricki immediately introduced himself to the twin substitutes in spectacular style.

Brain sent a head-high cross into the Rovers' penalty area and Ricki met it with an acrobatic bicycle-kick. It took everyone by surprise.

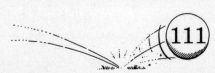

Mesmerized by the whirling limbs, the keeper never moved a muscle as Ricki made perfect contact and the ball zipped past him into the net.

It was a stunning goal. And before Rovers could recover, their lead was reduced even further. Luke accepted a pass from Ricki on the edge of the area, thought about having a shot himself, but wisely ruled it out and toe-poked the ball forward instead to set Gregg up for a simple second.

Against any other side, the Swifts might perhaps have gone on to win. They were playing well enough to cause such a shock. But Ridgeway Rovers were just too good a team to let that happen. Encouraged by their large home support, the Rovers managed to weather the storm and regain their grip on the game – mainly by trying to keep Ricki out of it.

The Rovers were also fitter than the Swifts. Although Ricki was still charging around, the others were feeling the strain. The great comeback had taken a heavy toll on their energies and as they tired, gaps opened up in the team's defences and Rovers helped themselves to two more late goals.

Luke's weary commentary attempted to sum up their looming 5–2 defeat philosophically.

'End of the road for the Swifts in the cup. End of a dream, too – but there's always next year. Football's all about winning and losing. You have to learn to accept both. You can't win 'em all, as they say . . .'

Brain overheard him. 'Never mind, Skipper. At least we're starting to win *some*. Shows we must be getting better.'

'Bang goes my New Year resolution, though,' Luke sighed.

'One out of two ain't so bad,' the winger grinned.

Luke brightened up. 'That's true. Now we're out the cup, we can concentrate on the league. We've still got a relegation battle to win!'

The skipper found some comfort again in Kipling's famous lines:

'If you can dream – and not make dreams your master,
If you can think – and not make thoughts your aim,
If you can meet with Triumph and Disaster,
And treat those two impostors just the same,
You'll be a man, my son!'

He felt his players had all grown up a bit after

such a performance – especially in self-respect and confidence. Luke looked at them proudly as the final whistle blew. They were exhausted, but still smiling in defeat. They knew they'd given it their best shot. And that was a kind of triumph.

'Nobody will be able to call us Luke's Flukes any more now,' he murmured in satisfaction.

THE END

CRAWFORD'S CORNER

Hi! Luke here. They've let me have a few pages of my own at last – and about time too! All footballers need a bit of space to really express themselves. Oops! Just split an infinitive there. 'Do I not like that!' as my English teacher might say sarcastically. (She knows I plan to be a commentator and soccer journalist when my playing career is over.)

Anyway, what they want me to do is write about the different team formations that I devised for the Swifts in this book. Hope you enjoyed it, by the way. We were dead unlucky in the end, don't you think? Still, that's football. It's a funny old game, as the saying goes.

Glad to have the chance to tell you more about it all. You might even like to try out a couple of these formations in the teams you play for. (Of course, it helps if you're the skipper, player-manager and

coach, too, like me, otherwise the Boss – or perhaps the teacher – might get narked if you start re-organizing the players without consulting them.) Failing that, you could always practise with your Subbuteo teams. Baffle your opponents with your cunning, new line-up!

While I'm on the subject, I thought I'd also go into the history of the way formations have developed over the years. I've been consulting my footie reference books and it's dead interesting. Well, at least I think so. I'm not called a walking soccer encyclopedia for nothing, you know.

Nowadays on TV, you'll hear the pundits ranting on about 4-4-2, 4-2-4, 4-3-3 and 3-5-2 formations, flat back fours, sweepers, split strikers, wing-backs and even the Christmas Tree. They can't always fit the various patterns on to the screen properly when they show the teams – and even then it's often calculated guesswork, trying to read the manager's mind.

For most of the twentieth century, however, up till about the 1950s, every team played with the same system. It's known as the WM formation because if you joined up the dots between the

players on paper, so to speak, you could make those letters. They always wore numbers from 1 to 11, too, not 35 or whatever that huge squads have today. Numbers really meant something then. They told you the player's exact position on the pitch, some of them unheard of now, and even the kind of player he was.

Wingers were usually small, nippy dribblers, hugging the touchline; inside-forwards tended to be skilful ball players; wing-halves were rugged, hard tackling men with cannonball shots; full-backs stayed in their own half, kicked the winger into the crowd and hoofed the ball upfield; centre-forwards were big, brave, powerful men who could run through a brick wall; and centre-halves were built with tree trunks for legs and with necks just as thick for heading the old, heavy, leather footballs.

As for the goalkeepers, they were *well* crazy in those days. They had to be. Few of them still had their own teeth, but collected those of centre-forwards instead when their punch missed the ball. It was too risky to try and catch it. They'd get barged into the net along with the ball!

Teams would line up like this in that WM shape:

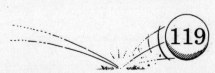

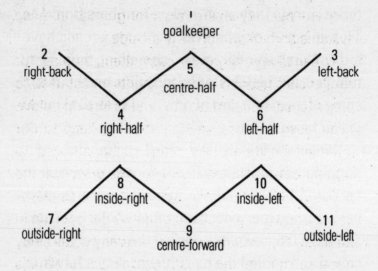

goalkeeper

2
right-back

5
centre-half

3
left-back

4
right-half

6
left-half

8
inside-right

10
inside-left

7
outside-right

9
centre-forward

11
outside-left

The wing-halves (defenders) and inside-forwards (attackers) were sort of midfield men, but the term hadn't been invented then. Midfielders only came into existence as teams began to experiment with more imaginative line-ups. The legendary Brazilians, with Pele in his famous number ten shirt, won the World Cup in 1958 and 1962 using the 4-2-4 arrangement. They weren't playing with only ten men of course – although this

120

lot might well have been able to win without a keeper – but goalies are taken for granted in these systems and aren't normally included.

Other teams began to copy them, hoping for similar success, and Swillsby Swifts in fact used to play a loose 4-2-4 formation, like the line-up below. I say loose because we don't tend to keep to our intended positions. (As skipper, I'm allowed to wander all over the pitch, popping up wherever the action is.) Unfortunately, we're not quite as clever as the Brazilians and all too often we got overrun in midfield. That meant we gave too many goals away because our defence just couldn't cope. (That's another way of saying that they weren't good enough to keep the ball out of our net, but don't tell them I said that!)

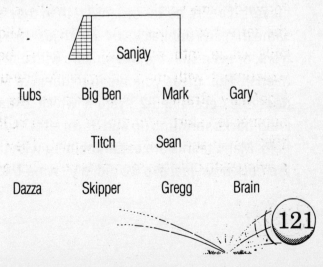

Sanjay

Tubs   Big Ben   Mark   Gary

Titch   Sean

Dazza   Skipper   Gregg   Brain

Then in 1966, Alf Ramsey came up with 4-3-3 to win the World Cup for England in the Geoff Hurst hat-trick final at Wembley (see this story for more exciting details). He only used this style of play as he reckoned he hadn't got any decent wingers so his team were called the Wingless Wonders. What that did, apart from earning Sir Alf a knighthood, was show that managers need to adapt their tactics to suit their own players – or to deal with the strengths and weaknesses of the opposition.

After that, playing 4-3-3 became more fashionable because managers realized you had a greater chance of dominating a game by putting an extra player in midfield. The theory is that if you can't outplay 'em, outnumber 'em! That way, even the Swifts can possibly beat a team with more talented players if we're better organized than they are. The same thinking applies to 4-4-2 with just two men up front, or even split the two strikers with one playing deeper. That gives you five in midfield at times, as does the recent 3-5-2 system which usually has wing-backs sprinting up and down either side of the field. Many teams are experimenting with three-at-the-back now, just like we did, plus wing-backs who

have that double job to do.

In the Euro '96 Championships, the England coach, Terry Venables, came so close to glory by boldly choosing attack-minded wingers as sort of wing-backs instead of defenders. He also invented the Christmas Tree, a formation that tapers to the front of the team, 4-3-2-1, like the shape of the traditional pine tree. It's a flexible system, giving you plenty of men around the ball in midfield and lots of attacking options too.

Just imagine this as a dream team, using the Christmas Tree: (I've stood the tree up the right way, using the goalie as the plant pot!)

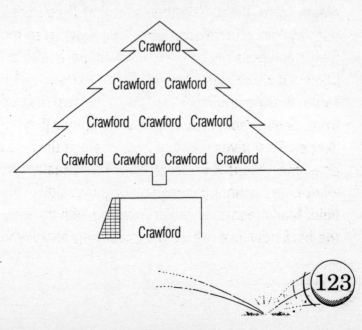

A team like that – with a bit of luck – could take on the world! Only dreaming, sadly. If only I was as good a player as cousin Jon. IF . . . Now that's a very big word. It's all right knowing the theory – it's doing it on the pitch I find so tricky. Just have to keep working on those skills.

See you again soon, I hope. Enjoy your footie!

Luke

ROB CHILDS
FOOTBALL DAFT

ILLUSTRATED BY
AIDAN POTTS

Especially for dyslexic readers

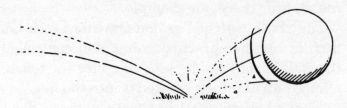

1 Shooting Practice

'No, no, no!' screamed the sports teacher. 'Go and fetch it – run!'

'Frosty' Winter struggled to keep hold of his temper – especially when the boy went and fell over the ball as he tried to dribble it back.

'Look, how many times have I told you, lad?' Frosty ranted. 'It's no good shooting from outside the area like that. You can't even get your shots on target from three metres, never mind thirty!'

Luke Crawford put on his best pained expression. He thought Frosty's criticism was a mite exaggerated. He'd been no more than twenty-five metres out at the most. 'But, you see, sir . . .' he began.

'I haven't got time for any of your rambling excuses,' the teacher cut in. 'Just leave the shooting to people who *can* shoot, OK? Like your cousin over there, for example.'

They both watched as Jon Crawford took his turn in another practice group. Jon controlled the ball in his stride with one elegant touch, glanced up and then stroked it into the net.

'That's how to do it! But you can't – so don't even try!' snapped Frosty. The teacher slouched away to find another hapless victim, leaving Luke to grin somewhat sheepishly at the other players in his group.

'Bit cruel, that,' said Gregg. 'Over the top, I'd say.'

'Yeah, but that's where Luke's effort went, too,' sniggered Gregg's identical twin, Gary. 'Right over the top of the goal!'

'I don't know how you put up with Frosty's sarcasm, Luke,' said Gregg. 'Why do you keep coming when it's obvious he doesn't want you here?'

'Simple. I want to play in the school team.'

'But he never picks you.'

'He does sometimes – when he has no other choice!'

'You're football daft, you are, Luke!' laughed Gary. 'I'd have thought being skipper, player-manager and coach of the Swifts would be enough for anybody, but you still want to play for the Comp as well!'

'Somebody has to. And I've got an even better chance now, haven't I?'

That was true. Frosty was facing a rebellion. Three boys had already dropped out of Swillsby Comprehensive's small Year 8 soccer squad, fed up of Frosty's black moods. Now he was in danger of losing his captain.

Matthew Clarke had failed to attend the last two training sessions, giving flimsy excuses, and this time had not bothered to tell the teacher at all. As Frosty fished the practice balls out of the sports store, he overheard the twins gossiping outside.

'Has Matt gone straight home?' asked Gregg.

'Yep,' replied Gary. 'Said he was only going to play Sunday football for the Panthers. Reckoned the Comp's got even worse than the Swifts!'

'Oh, come on, the school team isn't *that* bad yet.'

11

Gary grinned. 'And we should know – we play for both!'

Frosty was incensed. 'Right, if Clarke's not interested, then neither am I!' he seethed. 'No individual is bigger than the team. We'll just have to do without him.'

Luke's group had their attention refocused on the matter in hand by the demands of their goalkeeper. 'C'mon, you lot!' cried Sanjay. 'Whose go is it? I'm freezing standing here while you're all rabbiting on.'

'I'll warm old Dracula up,' Gregg smiled, using their pet nickname for the eccentric Sanjay Mistry who kept goal for Swillsby Swifts and the

Comp. If his bizarre behaviour between the posts didn't startle the opposition, it certainly scared the life out of his teammates!

Gregg tapped the ball a little way ahead of him and let fly from the edge of the penalty area. The shot had pace but, sadly, not the accuracy Gregg had intended, and Sanjay mocked him unmercifully.

'Looks like you getting warmed up, junior,' Gary chuckled, rubbing in his big brother status, being ten minutes older. 'Go on, chase after it!'

'Why did I have to get lumbered with you dummies?' the goalie moaned in jest. 'I've hardly had a save to make yet.'

'That's only because you've let everything past you,' Gary teased him.

'I couldn't even reach most of 'em!'

Big Ben collected another spare ball to try his luck. 'Reckon Frosty's deliberately put us Swifts together so we don't mess up his other groups,' he remarked. 'He thinks we're all useless.'

'He's right as well,' put in Tubs, the Swifts' overweight full-back.

'You speak for yourself,' Gary replied.

'OK, let's see how wonderful you are.'

'Big Ben's before me. He can show us how it's done.'

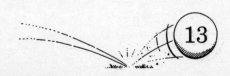

13

'Remember I haven't got my specs on,' the defender smiled, but he did at least manage to trouble Sanjay. The goalkeeper had to walk over and bend down to pick up his trickling, mis-hit slice.

'Thanks, Big Ben. Nice to have the ball in my hands again, just to remind me what it feels like.'

'C'mon, then, Gary, your turn,' said Big Ben as the goalkeeper threw the ball back towards the group. 'Smash one in and shut him up.'

Gary worked the ball onto his favoured left foot, took aim and fired, low and hard. But his shot was much too near the keeper and Sanjay merely stuck out his leg to knock it away.

'Couldn't be bothered to dive,' Sanjay laughed. 'Too easy!'

'Right, save this belter, then,' cried Tubs, hoping to fool him with a side-footer instead of thumping the ball in his usual toe-end style.

Sanjay treated his tame trundler with contempt, leaning on the post as the ball bobbled wide. 'Is that the best you people can do?' he snorted. 'You've all had three goes now and nobody's managed to score.'

Luke resolved to set a captain's example. Surrounded by so many Swifts, it felt as though

he was running his weekly practice with his own Sunday League side. He was determined to score. To make sure, he unwittingly took Frosty's advice and pushed the ball nearer and nearer the goal to give Sanjay no chance.

'Come closer, why don't you?' Sanjay taunted him, standing calmly on his goal-line. 'Are we gonna shake hands before you shoot?'

Luke almost reached the six-yard box before he pulled the trigger – but the gun blew up in his face. Somehow the ball got trapped between his feet and he skewed the shot wildly across the face of the goal. As he sank to his knees in

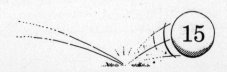

disbelief, the rest collapsed in hilarity, bringing their shooting practice to an abrupt and sloppy end.

By contrast, Frosty finished the session with an intensive game of two-touch football in the training grids, demanding maximum effort and concentration. Despite the fact that he was a well-qualified, experienced soccer coach, Frosty was never the most tolerant of teachers. Today, after the business over Matthew, he was more grumpy than normal with anybody who made a mistake. Even Jon, their leading scorer, felt the rough edge of his tongue when he attempted only a half-hearted tackle to win the ball.

'Get in the game more, lad!' Frosty yelled at him. 'You're bone-idle sometimes. What's the use of having all those skills on the ball if you don't get it in the first place?'

Luke feared that his cousin was going to respond with one of his casual little shrugs of the shoulders. And when Jon did go and do exactly that, Luke waited for the explosion.

He didn't have to wait long. The volcano blew its top almost instantly and Jon was sent back to the changing rooms. 'Go on!' Frosty roared. 'Off home you go as well and join our dear captain in front of the telly!'

16

As Jon trailed away, still in a daze about what he'd done wrong, the game continued in near silence. Even the bubbly Luke was subdued, upset by his talented cousin's humiliating treatment. Jon's laid-back style of play might make it appear as if he didn't care, but Luke knew that wasn't the case. Unlike himself, Jon was just too cool to let it show how much he really loved his football.

'Brilliant, Frosty, there goes our best player,' Luke murmured bitterly under his breath. 'Serves you right if I'm the only one left soon – and then you'll have to pick me!'

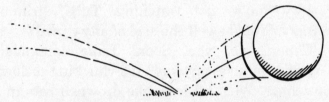

2 Running Commentary

'Right, men,' cried Luke, poised at the door of the changing hut to lead his team out on to the pitch. 'All ready?'

'Ready, Skipper!' the Swifts called back as usual to humour their captain, avoiding each other's eyes to prevent any outbreak of the giggles.

'Er . . . I'm not, Skipper, hang on a minute,' appealed Sean, Swifts' left-side midfielder. 'I've not finished combing my hair yet.'

There were groans all round. 'What a poser!' cackled Sanjay. 'He must reckon the crowd's here just to admire his hairstyle!'

Tubs glanced out through a hole in the wooden planking. 'Crowd! He calls five and a half people a crowd?'

'Half?' queried Luke, impatiently. 'Titch is in here with us!'

'Oh, no, sorry, it's your dad. He's just stood up!'

'Pity you're not watching, Tubs,' grinned Sanjay. 'You'd swell the size of any crowd!'

'C'mon, will you, Sean!' Luke demanded. 'What's the use, anyway? It's chucking it down out there. We'll all look like drowned rats in a minute.'

'It's not exactly dry in here,' grumbled Titch. 'There's a leak in the roof over me.'

'S.O.S.,' cried Tubs. 'Titch is getting washed away.'

'Need a tidal wave to carry you off,' Titch said, adding to the friendly insults hurling about the ramshackle hut.

Luke sometimes wished his players would approach a vital league match a little more seriously. Especially with the looming prospect of relegation. He tried again to recapture their attention, tapping the logo on the front of his gold shirt. 'OK, team. Let's make this another *GREAT GAME*!'

'For them or for us?' grunted Brain,

their disorganized left-winger.

Luke stared at him. 'You've got odd socks on again!'

Brain gazed down at his mixed pair of gold and red socks. 'Yeah, soz, Skipper. In a bit of a hurry this morning.'

Luke closed his eyes and offered up a quick, silent prayer for mercy. He knew they would certainly need some extra help from somewhere. Despite the state of the home team's changing hut and the ridiculous name they'd given themselves, Real Marwood demanded respect. They were the league's top scorers and pushing hard for promotion.

Real were not in the mood to let either the heavy rain or the feeble opposition distract them from their ambitions. Their manager screamed his nonstop instructions from the touchline, displaying a colourful, if limited, vocabulary. And when Real scored the opening goal, he jumped about as though somebody had put a firework down his trousers.

The Swifts' adult duo, by contrast, showed all the animation of a damp squib, huddled under Luke's uncle's large umbrella. 'Don't know why our lads always look so amazed when they let a

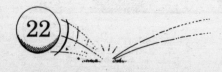

goal in,' Uncle Ray commented wryly. 'You'd think they'd be used to it.'

Luke's dad glanced up at his bearded younger brother. 'That's down to Luke, I reckon,' he said. 'He keeps telling them so often how much they're improving that maybe they're beginning to believe him.'

Ray chuckled. 'Doubt it. More likely they're not fully aware just how bad they really are!'

'That's a bit harsh. The main thing is, they're still enjoying their football. Results aren't everything, you know.'

'Good job, or the manager and coach might have got the sack by now.'

'Who, us? But we don't do anything. We leave it all to Luke.'

'Exactly!' grinned Ray. 'Just look at him now, charging around as if the future of the world was at stake.'

They gazed at Luke, partly in admiration and partly in pity, as the number nine chased the ball all over the pitch. His hyperactivity was occasionally rewarded with the odd kick, sometimes in the wrong direction, but everybody knew if the Swifts' skipper was anywhere near. They would pick up this buzzing sound in their

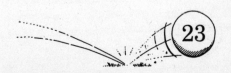

ears, as irritating as radio interference. It was Luke's habitual running commentary.

'The Swifts need to hit back quickly after Real's lucky first goal. Inspired by their skipper, who's involved in every move, they launch a dangerous raid down the left wing where Brain has the beating of his marker. Brain shows him the ball then whips it away out of reach, slipping it inside to the skipper in space . . .'

Sadly, Luke wasn't in as much space as he thought. Carried away by his biased commentary, he didn't know there was a defender trotting along behind him. The ball slid under

his boot to his laughing opponent and with barely a pause, Luke turned and raced off again in pursuit.

'*Robbed of possession by a wicked bobble on the bumpy, rain-sodden pitch, the skipper doubles back to get ball-side again, tireless as ever in supporting his players. Wherever they look to find him and help them out of trouble, Luke Crawford is there . . .*'

In reality, outside Luke's world of fantasy football, it meant that he was liable to pop up anywhere to get in their way. Not by coincidence, the Swifts' only worthwhile shot of the first half

managed to escape Luke's intervention. Brain's jinking solo run took him skilfully through three challenges, but he saw his low drive well saved by the otherwise unemployed home keeper.

Sanjay was kept somewhat busier. The ball that beat him for the fourth goal skimmed over the wet grass like a flat stone across a lake before its loopy trajectory finally eluded his flailing arms.

'Four–nil!' groaned Dazza, the right-winger, as they all tried to creep under Ray's umbrella at half-time. 'I've hardly touched the ball yet.'

'Lucky you,' said Big Ben. 'Us defenders haven't had a second's rest. Why don't you come back and help out if you're so bored?'

'I'm ready for a breakaway, aren't I? You tell 'em, Skip.'

'That's right,' Luke confirmed. 'We can't give up hope of scoring and getting back into this game, men . . .'

Gary cut in. Luke hadn't succeeded in giving a team talk all season without being interrupted. 'What do you mean, getting *back* into the game? We've never even been in it once yet!'

'Well, it's about time we were, then, isn't it?' Luke replied. 'Let's try and give *them* something to worry about for a change . . .'

'Like whether they're gonna be able to reach double figures or not,' suggested Tubs.

'Rubbish!' Luke scoffed. 'They're not going to score ten against us.'

Luke was right. Real Marwood had rattled up *twelve* goals by the time the referee's whistle piped its last soggy peep and saved the Swifts from further punishment. The second half was a fiasco – from Titch's deflected own goal to Sean's late decision to duck out of the way of a goal-bound screamer.

'Not going to head that one,' Sean said. 'Might have given me a second parting on the wrong side!'

'I'll part your hair again for you,' Sanjay growled, sitting in a muddy puddle. 'With an axe!'

The only silver lining in the Swifts' storm clouds was their single goal. It came as a mere consolation when they were already so far behind that not even the Real manager could bother to utter more than a couple of curses in response to criticize his team's slack marking.

'Dazza and Gregg have linked up well down the right, playing a clever one-two that the coach has shown them in training. Now Dazza swings over a low cross into the middle. Who's there to

meet it? It's Brain . . .'

Luke broke out of his commentary mode in alarm. 'Brain!' he gasped. 'What's *he* doing there? I told him to stay out on the wing!'

Brain connected with a classic, right-foot volley, high off the ground. It almost gave the keeper a ricked neck with the speed that the ball flew past him to billow out the netting.

'Fantastic goal!' Gregg whooped. 'A blinder. The school team could do with a few like that.'

Luke wandered back alone to the halfway line, lost in thought. 'Hmm, you're dead right there, Gregg. They could indeed . . .'

The Swifts' captain was so preoccupied, he went automatically to the centre-spot and prepared to kick off again.

'Don't you reckon you've done that enough today?' smirked Real's centre-forward, already with four of his side's goals to his credit. 'Let us have a go for a change, eh? I haven't scored from here yet!'

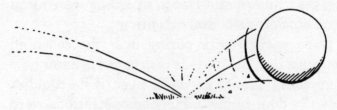

3 Want to Play?

The sports hall of Swillsby Comprehensive echoed to the sounds of pounding feet, shouts and footballs smacking against its walls. It wasn't any of the school teams doing extra training on a dark Wednesday evening, but the Swifts hard at work improving their soccer skills.

At least that was the general idea behind Luke persuading Dad to book the hall for an hour each week during the winter. He'd even had Uncle Ray filming the first few sessions so that the players could study their own techniques on video tape.

Sadly, as with most of Luke's ideas, things tended not to go quite to plan. The players were too busy enjoying a good kick-about to pay much heed to his coaching – and the filming stopped after a stray pass from Dazza hit Ray on the head and made him drop the camcorder. Head, glasses, camera and Dazza's passing were all in need of some remedial attention.

Luke spent hours poring over the coaching manuals that littered his bedroom. He knew how everything should be done, even if he couldn't actually do it himself. His demonstrations were always eagerly awaited.

'Look,' he began, halting a group practising their chipping. 'You have to make sure you get more underneath the ball to lift it . . .'

'Titch is the only one here who could get *underneath* the ball, Skip,' put in Dazza quickly, deliberately trying to sidetrack him.

Luke pressed on regardless. 'If you place your non-kicking foot just there, see, and lean back . . .'

This time it was Gary who interrupted him. 'Where was that again?'

'Just there,' repeated Luke, showing them once more. 'If you place your left foot well behind the ball, then with your right . . .'

'But I kick with my left foot, remember,' Gary persisted. 'I only use the right one for standing on!'

Luke sighed, realizing what they were up to. 'OK, just do everything the opposite way to what I'm saying.'

'Oh, that's easy, then,' Gary grinned. 'I do that anyway!'

'Just watch me,' said Luke, hoping to appear confident. 'This is how to chip a ball to a team-mate over somebody's head.'

He took a few steps back from the ball and

then paused. 'I'll aim to chip it about as high as that basketball ring on the wall, right?'

'Right, Skipper,' they nodded, trying to look serious.

Luke trotted in, picturing in his mind the illustrations from the books that made it seem so simple. Unfortunately he misjudged his run-up and plonked his left foot down too far behind the ball. He had to overstretch to reach it and slipped, toppling backwards as the ball trickled mockingly across the tiled floor.

Luke hauled himself to his feet with as much dignity as he could muster in the circumstances, ignoring the stifled giggles. 'Yes, well, it does take a bit of practice to get it right,' he said, giving a little cough. 'But that's what we're here for, isn't it?'

'That's true, Skipper,' grinned Big Ben. 'Would you . . . er . . . just show us again what you did. I'm not quite certain how to break my fall safely when I try to copy that!'

Luke shot him a dirty look. 'Brain!' he called out. 'Come over here a minute, will you, and show these clodhoppers how to chip a ball properly.'

'Which foot, Skipper?' Brain asked.

'Either, doesn't matter.'

'Good, 'cos I'm never sure which is which,' Brain admitted.

'Just wish more of us had two good feet like you,' Luke said in genuine envy.

'Yeah, as long as you don't try and kick with both at the same time,' Dazza cackled.

Brain did what came naturally to him. He'd never read a coaching book in his life. In fact, he'd barely read any book in his life. With his dyslexic difficulties, he struggled to make sense of even the most basic sentences on his bad days.

This was one of his good ones. He chipped the first ball with his slightly stronger left foot, making perfect contact to send the ball slapping high against the far wall. He changed the angle of his approach for the next demonstration, using his other foot. This time the ball curled up and, to everyone's sheer amazement, thudded into the backboard and plopped down through the basketball ring.

'Did you mean to do that?' gasped Gary.

Brain grinned and shook his head. 'Course not. Sliced that one a bit. Bet I couldn't do it again if I stood here and tried all night.'

'OK, see if the rest of you can,' said Luke,

seizing the opportunity to give them some incentive. 'I just want a little word with old Brain here.'

He took the winger to one side of the hall to sit on a bench. 'I've been thinking . . .' Luke began.

'Oh, oh! I'm not sure I'm gonna like the sound of this,' said Brain.

'No, listen, would you like to play a bit more football each week?'

'How can I when the Swifts play every Sunday?'

'I mean for the school,' said Luke. 'Why don't you come and play for the Comp as well? We need someone like you.'

'*We?*' he queried. 'I didn't know you played in the school team.'

'Well, not every game,' Luke smiled, bending the truth to suit his own purpose. 'But we're not doing very well this season, and having you on the wing would be great. Might make all the difference.'

Brain shook his head. 'Soz, Skipper. I'm not gonna suffer all Frosty's snide comments again. I went to a few practices in the first year and he used to get at me something rotten.'

'Yes, but you're loads better now. Look how well you've been playing for the Swifts.'

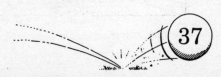

37

Brain stood up and started to walk away. 'Ta for the offer,' he said, turning back for a moment. 'I like playing for the Swifts and I don't want Frosty to go and spoil things. I nearly gave up soccer altogether 'cos of him.'

'Well, I did try,' Luke sighed as Brain rejoined his group. 'Perhaps I'll have another go at him after he's thought it over for a few days.'

Luke organized the players into a six-a-side game of two-touch football – a very optimistic ruling when most of them usually needed half a dozen attempts to control a ball. They did their best, however, playing with an enthusiasm that would do credit to a team at the top of the league. Their 12–1 defeat was never mentioned. It was taken for granted; they were half-expecting another thrashing next Sunday as well from whoever they were up against.

After Luke blazed a shot over Sanjay's low crossbar, Uncle Ray managed to catch his attention. 'Somebody to see you,' he growled, hoicking a thumb in the direction of the door.

'Frosty!' Luke gulped. 'What's he doing here?'

'No idea, but I'm not speaking to that chap at the moment. Jon came home today and told me Frosty's gone and dropped him for Saturday's match. The man must be an idiot.'

'He is,' nodded Luke. 'Jon's not exactly flavour of the month with him right now after what happened last week.'

'Aye, I know. Thought it'd all blow over, but it seems Frosty wants to make a point. Get rid of him quick, will you, before I say something I might regret.'

Luke strolled across to the teacher. 'Hello, sir, come to spy on us, have you, and pick up a few tips?'

'You must be joking!' rasped Frosty. 'I'm surprised to see you lot here. Just popped back to pick up something I'd left behind and I couldn't believe my eyes.'

'Why's that, sir?'

'You mean the Swifts actually practise?' Frosty said, and Luke could tell he was building up to one of his so-called witticisms. 'Amazing! Didn't know you had to practise so hard at being so bad!'

Luke decided to remain silent, tempted though he was to point out that the school team's results this season had been little better. After all, he should know. Luke was obsessed with keeping soccer statistics. He recorded full details in his little black notebooks, not only of every Swifts' match, but of the school team's too.

'Anyway,' Frosty said, changing the subject and looking a shade embarrassed. 'I was going to ask you tomorrow, but seeing as you're here now, well . . .'

Luke waited patiently, enjoying the teacher's obvious discomfort. 'It's just that we are . . . um . . . a bit short-staffed, like,' Frosty stumbled on, 'and I was wondering if you were doing anything on Saturday morning . . .'

Frosty trailed away, leaving Luke to draw his own conclusions. 'You mean, you want me to be a sub in the league match against St Paul's?'

Frosty shuffled his feet and gave a sort of sheepish leer. 'Actually, I was thinking about playing you right from the start. Reckon you deserve the chance in a way, attending every practice like you do.'

Luke drew in a sharp breath. This was music to his ears. He'd only ever been included in the Comp's starting line-up once before – and he preferred to draw a veil over that personal disaster.

He swallowed hard before trusting his voice to reply. 'Yes, I think I'll be free to play that day, sir!' he said simply.

What he really wanted to do was to jump up

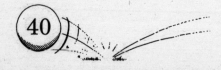

and down, clench his fists in delight and run
about the hall, shouting at the top of his voice,
'I'm in! I'm in! I've finally made it!'

That would have to wait until he was by
himself later . . .

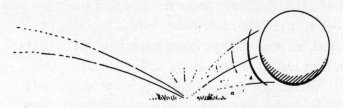

4 From Bad to Worse

'And now here's Luke Crawford, the Comp's new striker, promoted into the First Team in their hour of need. He's ghosted deep into the Saints' penalty area and nobody's picked him up. If only Swillsby can get the ball to him. The deadly number nine just doesn't miss chances like this . . .'

Luke not only did miss the chance when it came, he totally missed the ball as well. Gary had spotted Luke lurking by the far post, unmarked, and swung over a long cross towards him. The full-back merely hoped for the best – but feared the worst. And so it proved.

Luke had been left unmarked for two reasons. Firstly, because St Paul's were already 5–0 up and rapidly losing interest in the contest – and secondly, because their defenders had already written off the number nine as posing no threat. The ball sailed over their heads and Luke rose to meet it, eyes firmly closed. His jump was so ill-timed, he would have been too late even to make contact with the ball in an action replay.

What his subsequent untidy landing lacked in artistic merit, it more than made up for in comic effect. Luke sprawled full-length in a pool of dirty water as if he had just belly-flopped in a race at a swimming gala.

He picked himself up out of the mire, his black and white striped shirt now looking more like it belonged to an All Blacks rugby team.

'Penalty!' Luke appealed. 'Somebody pushed me as I jumped.'

'There was nobody near you, lad,' Frosty growled back, wishing he could blow the whistle instead for full time. The weakened Comp side had been completely outplayed by the visitors, and the teacher could just imagine the gleeful reaction of Matthew and co. when they heard the result. The very thought of it made his teeth ache!

Matthew had been openly forecasting an annihilation all week. 'Without me and you, Adam, the Comp's gonna get murdered!' he chortled to his Padley Panthers' teammate.

'And Jon,' Adam reminded him. 'Frosty's gone and lost all three of his Panthers' stars now.'

'Yeah, careless of him,' Matthew grinned. 'He'll have to come begging on his hands and knees before I might consider playing for the Comp again!'

'Me too,' said Adam, looking at the team sheet on the sports noticeboard. 'He must be desperate. Half of this lot are Swifts!'

Matthew could not contain his mirth. 'Well, if there's one thing Loony Luke's Sloths are good at, it's getting thrashed!'

Sanjay and the Garner twins were the only Swifts to be regulars for the school too. Even that, Gary believed, was because Frosty couldn't tell him and Gregg apart so didn't know which one to drop. Now they had been joined by Luke, Big Ben and Tubs to make up the numbers. The Swifts almost felt at home as the score mounted up against them.

'Still time to get a goal or two back ourselves, Gregg,' Luke insisted as the sixth flashed past Sanjay. 'Never give up.'

Gregg shook his head in admiration. 'Somehow you always look on the bright side of any disaster. You'd make the sinking of the *Titanic* sound like a good chance to practise lifeboat drill!'

Luke was simply relieved that, for once, he had not been the cause of the crushing defeat. He had after all only given one penalty away so far.

'*Just a few minutes left of a one-sided match, but Luke Crawford refuses to give up hope,*' droned his commentary. '*He wins the ball back in midfield, but his pass catches Tubs sleeping*

46

and a Saints striker is through on goal. Sanjay comes out to narrow the angle – oh, dear! Seven–nil.'

That was it. Frosty could stand no more. He blew the whistle early and stomped off in disgust back to the school building. They had another match coming up the following week – in the cup – and he had no idea what kind of a team he was going to be able to put out.

The prospect of reinstating Matthew stuck in his craw. Jon Crawford, though, was another matter, and Frosty suspected he had perhaps

acted rather too hastily there. He might well have to swallow his pride . . .

As the players trailed in after him, Luke caught sight of a spectator standing over by the hedge. 'Hi, Brain, how long have you been watching?'

Brain shrugged. 'Dunno, I missed the start.'

'Pity you weren't on the pitch,' Luke said. 'Why don't you change your mind and give it a go next week? I'm sure Frosty would jump at you.'

'Probably jump *on* me,' Brain replied. 'He always used to.'

'C'mon, he's not that bad,' Luke began to argue, but stopped as Brain pulled a face. 'Well, maybe he is, I admit, but things have changed. Right now, old Frosty needs every extra player he can get.'

'I'll think about it.'

'Good man, and don't forget – tomorrow morning, quarter past ten at the changing cabin. Swifts versus the Wanderers.'

'Yeah, don't worry, I'll be there.'

At kick-off time next day, the Swifts were a player short. Their one and only sub had cried off and Brain had still not reported for duty.

48

'Where's he got to?' Luke fumed as Uncle Ray went to fetch him. 'Bet he's still trying to find his shorts or something. Typical!'

'He can't help it, you know, Skipper,' Titch said. 'He's just like that, always losing and forgetting things, getting himself muddled up.'

'I know,' Luke sighed. 'But we actually had a chance of a result here against the Wanderers. They're in relegation trouble as well.'

After a heavy overnight frost, the referee had inspected the pitch very carefully before allowing the match to go ahead. 'Best to wear all-weather trainers with extra grip, if you've got them,' he advised the players as they changed in the cabin. 'Anybody in studded boots is going to find it difficult to turn without slipping over.'

'Play the way you're facing,' Luke told his team. 'Keep it simple. Don't try anything too fancy on this surface.'

'No danger of that from us,' said Tubs, giving his distinctive, rumbling laugh. 'These conditions ought to suit us. Bring the other lot down to our level!'

Luke didn't like to agree openly, but privately thought the same. That is, until Brain failed to appear. He was such a key player for the Swifts and the source of most of their goals. The

realization that his teammates valued his abilities had done wonders for Brain's own confidence, too, and he had begun to believe in himself far more at last.

Before the game started, Sanjay jumped up to touch the crossbar as usual. It was meant to bring him luck, but any observer studying the Swifts' goals-against column in the league table might have been excused thinking otherwise. 'Glad I'm wearing my trackie bottoms today,' he murmured, stamping on the bone-hard, rutted goalmouth. 'Have to watch the bounce, though.

The ball's sure gonna do some crazy things on this.'

It was the state of the ground, in fact, that enabled Luke to put the ball into the net after just five minutes. Unfortunately, it was his own.

The ball ricocheted to the captain in a crowded Swifts' goalmouth but sat up awkwardly on one of the ruts as Luke attempted a mighty clearance. His wild swing resulted in the most horrendous slice off the outside of his trainer that sent the ball spiralling back over Sanjay's head. If Dracula's looks could kill, the team would have needed a new skipper!

Two minutes later, this time at the right end, Luke seemed to have made amends for his gross error. Dazza crossed the ball low into the Wanderers' area and a cruel bounce fooled everyone – until Luke stuck out a foot.

'*Goooaaalll!!! The skipper has equalized!*' blared out the ecstatic commentary as the scorer danced about the penalty area.

Even in his frenzy, the small part of Luke's mind that remained in gear began to wonder why none of his teammates were racing to join in his celebrations. They had all heard something that had failed to register on Luke's consciousness – the referee's whistle.

51

'Sorry, lad, no goal,' the official said, trying to calm him down. 'You were offside when the ball was passed.'

The bad news had the desired effect. Even Luke's commentary held a minute's silence to mark his grief – and this was extended further when the Wanderers went and increased their lead. Big Ben's centre-back partner, Mark, fell over at the wrong moment, allowing an attacker a clear sight of goal. Sanjay's lucky charm once again failed to work any magic.

It was at that moment that Brain finally made his appearance, scrambling out of Ray's car. 'Soz, guys,' he apologized. 'Must have misread my watch. Didn't realize what the time was.'

'Haven't you got any trainers?' whined Luke.

'Yeah, but I couldn't find them. Think I must have left them behind in the sports hall after our practice. Won't my boots be all right?'

Brain got his answer the first time the ball came out to him on the left wing. He tried a dummy shuffle to bamboozle his opponent and finished up on his backside as his feet slithered from underneath him.

Luke tried hard to keep any note of desperation out of his commentary.

'Can the Swifts just hold out till the interval to give their player-manager time to make some vital changes? Now at full strength at last, they might still stand a chance of winning this match – if only they can actually stand up!'

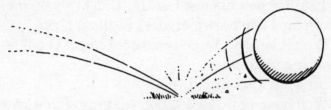

5 Swap!

'It's stupid playing on a frozen pitch like this,' Sean muttered at half-time. 'Somebody's going to end up with a broken leg.'

'Is that why I haven't seen you make a tackle yet?' Luke asked pointedly. 'It's been like playing with nine men, not ten.'

Sean affected a shrug. 'Well, I've got a date this afternoon and I don't want to have to turn up to it in a wheelchair.'

'A date!' snorted Tubs. 'He's only gonna hang around with a gang of kids outside the village hall, trying to look cool. I've seen 'em there.'

Sean had to suffer a chorus of jeers before Luke managed to focus minds back on the game. 'Look, Brain's side of the pitch second half isn't as bad as the other. Let's make the most of him now he's here and give him the ball as much as possible.'

Brain shook his head sadly. 'Don't rely on me, Skipper. I can't keep my feet in these boots.'

'You'll be OK,' Luke reassured him. 'You'll be wearing trainers.'

'I haven't got any, I told you.'

'You have now,' said Luke, yanking off his own shoes. 'Mine! C'mon, we both take the same size. Give me your boots and we'll do a swap.'

It was the ultimate sacrifice for the captain to make for the good of the team. Luke acknowledged that his own performance might suffer – though perhaps not to a degree that anyone else would notice – but Brain had the special ability that could well swing the match in their favour.

The Swifts responded to Luke's unselfish gesture and started the second half like a team possessed. They threw themselves into tackles to win the ball at all costs and supplied Brain with it at every opportunity.

Even Sean risked life and limb in support of Brain up and down the left flank. After ten minutes' play, he challenged strongly to win a fifty-fifty ball and then tried to exchange a quick one-two pass with Brain to get past a defender. The full-back refused to let them by, deliberately tripping Sean as he ran forward for Brain's return ball.

'Free-kick,' indicated the referee. 'Direct.'

That was all Luke wanted to hear. Standing over the ball to conduct operations, the captain displayed four fingers of his right hand behind his back to the waiting Brain. It was part of a secret signalling code Luke had worked out for use at dead-ball kicks like this, designed to keep the opposition guessing about their intentions.

It confused Brain too. He saw the sign but couldn't remember what it was supposed to mean. He never bothered to revise the code printed in Luke's dossier of tactics given out to every player in the squad. It was all too detailed for him.

As Luke suddenly darted to one side, losing his footing in the process, Brain gave a little shrug and ran in. He struck the ball fiercely, bang on target. It ripped clean through a hole in the defensive wall and powered into the net with the goalkeeper left gaping.

Luke sat on the frosty ground, muttering to himself, 'Four fingers, Brain, four fingers. That means try a curler round the wall, not blast the ball straight through it. Why don't you ever follow instructions?'

Any comeback hopes were almost halted in their tracks a minute later when a header crashed against the Swifts' crossbar. The ball bounced down and out again for Big Ben to clear.

'Over the line, ref!' appealed the Wanderers' captain. 'The ball crossed the line.'

'Not all of it,' ruled the referee, perfectly positioned to make his judgement. 'Sorry, no goal!'

58

'Phew!' breathed Titch. 'That makes up for your goal which didn't count, Skipper.'

'No, it doesn't,' Luke stated flatly. 'Nothing makes up for that!'

The Swifts had to survive a crucial period of heavy bombardment from the Wanderers. They were rescued once by a brave stop from Sanjay, risking his teeth in a dive among a mass of flying feet, and then by Tubs blocking a shot on the goal-line.

Sanjay grinned as he slapped Tubs on his broad back. 'No way past you, eh, pal? As good as boarding up my goal with wood!'

'Yeah, when Tubs stands in front of the sun, we get a total eclipse!' chortled Gary. 'No offence, of course, Tubs.'

'Good job or I'd knock the living daylights out of both of you,' Tubs responded, letting his laugh rumble on.

It was very much against the run of play, therefore, when the Swifts broke away to snatch the all-important equalizer.

'Sean brings the ball over the halfway line, moving into the space created by Luke Crawford's clever decoy run . . . Oops! The skipper's slipped, but Sean slides a killer pass

60

inside the full-back to Brain for the winger to shoot. Oohh! The goalie's saved it, but can't hold on to the ball. It runs loose to Dazza – Goooaaalll!!! Dazza has lashed the rebound high into the net. And now I hand you over to our summarizer . . .'

Luke was also the summarizer, but let his imaginary audience wait for further pearls of wisdom. He didn't want to miss out on the celebrations as Dazza's brilliant white smile lit up Swillsby recreation ground. The Swifts were back on level terms.

Neither team was good enough to conjure up any further goals before the final whistle, both being content in the end to avoid another defeat.

'Told you we could do it, men,' boasted Luke in the cabin afterwards. 'You've just got to have more faith in yourselves – and me!'

'Thanks for the loan of the trainers, Skipper,' said Brain, swapping them again for his boots. 'Er, I've been thinking . . .'

'That makes a nice change,' Luke quipped. 'Did you enjoy it?'

Brain giggled. 'You know what I mean.'

'About giving the school another go?'

Brain nodded. 'Might as well. Seeing as how

the Comp are struggling to raise a team. Didn't want to get shown up there, that's all.'

'No danger of that,' Luke confirmed. 'And no need to worry about Frosty either. You've shown how to cope with one kind of frostbite today, so now you can do it again!'

At home that evening Luke pondered over the successes of the day with quiet satisfaction. Sitting at the desk in his bedroom, he brought his notebook up to date, logging team details, ground conditions and scorers, all in red ink in his neat, small handwriting. It was a task he always looked forward to, even when the Swifts lost heavily, but it wasn't as much fun as composing the match report.

He began to draft out the report that would appear in the next issue of the *Swillsby Chronicle*, the village free newspaper edited by Uncle Ray. He let his nephew loose on the sports page every month to satisfy Luke's growing journalistic ambitions – even though Luke, of course, saw himself becoming a football reporter and television commentator only after his own professional playing career was over. In traditional tabloid style, Luke rarely let the facts get in the way of a good story.

Swifts 2 Wanderers 2

Swillsby Swifts earned another precious point with a spirited draw against fellow relegation strugglers, the Wanderers. On a treacherous, frosty pitch the battling Swifts – a man short – unluckily trailed 0–2 at half-time. Inspired by their player-manager, Luke Crawford, they fought back with goals from wingers Brian 'Brain' Draper and David 'Dazza' Richards. Luke was robbed of an early strike by a controversial offside decision, but shrugged off that disappointment and lent leading scorer Brain his magic goal-grabbing trainers. Brain repaid the unselfish skipper with a goal from a well-rehearsed free-kick routine, cunningly devised by the coach, and then made the later equalizer for Dazza. 'A fine team display,' said the modest skipper afterwards. 'It shows how much the Swifts have improved this season and we deserve to avoid the dreaded drop.'

Luke chewed the end of his pen thoughtfully for a minute before putting it down. 'Hmm, that should just about do it,' he murmured, tastefully omitting any mention of his own goal. 'But maybe an extra quote from the coach might be useful to include for the *Chronicle* piece . . .'

His mind wandered on to the school's forthcoming cup game. 'Huh! I find the Comp a new star player, and I bet Frosty won't even thank me for it,' he grunted. 'Just my luck as well if he goes and gives Brain my place in the team!'

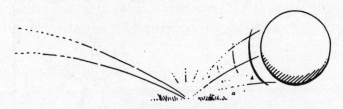

6 In and Out

It snowed the next day. And the next. And the day after that. The rumpled white duvet of snow covering the pitches put an untimely stop to any outdoor practices and the weekend fixtures also had to be cancelled.

Luke's face was as gloomy as the weather. 'Just when things were looking up as well,' he grumbled during a breather at the Swifts' midweek session in the sports hall. 'I reckon we were starting to hit our best form and I'd even managed to get picked for the Comp.'

'Pity!' Brain sympathized. 'I won't change my

mind, though. I still intend to go to Frosty's next practice.'

'Wonder if he'll have sorted things out with the rebels by then?' Gregg chipped in.

'Don't include my cousin with that lot. He was just an innocent victim of Frosty's bad temper,' Luke said. 'Anyway, it's all blown over now. Jon told me yesterday that Frosty has actually apologized for dropping him.'

'Never!' exclaimed Gregg.

Luke nodded. 'Straight up. Wish I'd been there. If I'd caught it on video, I could have made a fortune renting out the tape!'

'Maybe Ray threatened not to let his son play for the school again?'

Luke shrugged. 'It's just great that Jon's back. All star players have ups and downs in their careers, even the legendary Johan Cruyff!'

'The old Flying Dutchman is a real hero of yours, isn't he?' Brain grinned as Gregg chased off after a stray ball.

'Sure is. If I didn't already call my cousin Johan, I might even say you're a bit like the Maestro.'

'You're joking!'

'No, I'm not. The way you can shoot and cross a ball with either foot and dribble like a wizard, it's magic!'

'Thanks, makes a change to get a bit of praise,' said Brain. 'Matt was giving me a hard time again today, trying to show me up as usual.'

'Why was that?'

'Oh, you know Jenkins who takes us for maths? Well, he's been having a blitz on our tables recently and I still can't say them. I just get all muddled up and forget where I am.'

'What's that got to do with Matt?' asked Luke crossly. 'He's not exactly Einstein either when it comes to numbers!'

'Better than me, anyway. He kept coming out

with loud remarks about me being thick and stupid.'

'Didn't Jenkins stop him?'

'Pretended not to hear. I think he's a bit scared of Matt – always lets him get away with things, but not me.' Brain sighed and then added, 'Funny, they reckon he was a bit dyslexic, too, you know.'

'Who, Jenkins?'

'No, Einstein – and he was a genius!'

'Well, at least Miss Elliot in English knows you're not stupid. She often says what good ideas you come out with in discussions and that.'

'Yeah, but I can't get them down on paper, that's the trouble. Can't even spell my own name right sometimes. I don't realize I've got the letters the wrong way round until somebody like Matt makes fun of it.'

'Matt just likes picking on people,' Luke sighed. 'Does it to me as well 'cos he thinks I'm useless at football.'

Brain deliberately didn't say anything, even though Luke paused for a moment, hoping the winger might at least deny Matthew's judgement.

'Anyway,' Luke continued, 'I think Matt's bitten off more than he can chew if he's trying to

70

get the better of Frosty. Can't see Frosty backing down again. Guess he'll have to pick a new school team captain.'

Brain noticed a little gleam in Luke's eye. 'Don't go raising your hopes,' he said gently.

The melting snow was still lying on the ground in slushy patches when Frosty called an emergency practice session on the Tuesday of the following week. Only fourteen boys were present, including one new face – Brain.

'Pleased to see you here, Brian,' the teacher greeted him, using his proper name, as the boys wandered up to the pitch.

'You can call me Brain, if you like, sir. Most people do.'

'I prefer Brian,' said Frosty gruffly, but then made an effort to appear friendly. 'Heard you've been having a good season with the Swifts. Leading scorer, I gather. You ought to have come and joined us earlier.'

Brain realized that Luke must have been preparing the way in advance for his sudden appearance. 'Thought you had enough players,' he answered, 'but Luke said I might stand a fair chance of getting a game.'

'Well, Luke might be right for once. I'll

71

see what you can do first.'

Their opponents wanted to rearrange the cup game for Thursday afternoon but Frosty needed to check how many boys were available – and willing – to play. It would mean leaving school early that day.

'Thanks for attending at short notice,' Frosty said to the shivering group around him.

'Anything to have the chance of skipping off school early on Thursday,' laughed Gary. 'I'd be missing maths!'

Frosty actually smiled. 'Before we start the practice, I want you all to meet your new captain. The name's Crawford . . .'

For the briefest of moments, Luke's heart leapt into his mouth, but he did wonder later whether Frosty had done it on purpose – just to tease him.

'Jon Crawford!' Frosty announced after a theatrical pause and Jon grinned bashfully. 'Even if Matthew Clarke ever comes back into the squad, Jon's going to remain captain of the Comp team from now on.'

'Congrats, Johan,' Luke said as the players broke away to warm up. 'You should have been skipper in the first place. Matt was always too

quick to moan at anybody who made a mistake – especially me!'

'Don't worry, Luke,' Jon smiled. 'I won't be getting at you. Just play the best you can, that'll do me.'

Luke hugged himself with delight. With Jon as team captain, he looked forward with fresh optimism to a more regular place in the side, despite the extra competition from Brain. Inevitably, it was the new attacker who caught the eye – Frosty's eye.

The sports teacher didn't have Brain for Games and he was impressed – very impressed

indeed – with what he now saw. 'Can't believe how much this kid has come on since last year,' he muttered to himself.

Frosty was tempted to include Brain immediately in the cup team and his mind was made up in one flash of brilliance. The winger received the ball tight on the left touchline in the seven-a-side game, hemmed in by two players, but slipped through them with a touch of Houdini-like escapology. His quicksilver feet also tricked him past another tackle before he drew Sanjay out of goal and flicked it expertly over the keeper into the net.

Luke looked on like a proud father, assuming full credit for grooming such rare talent. 'Who needs Matthew Clarke now we've got Brain?'

Luke's question was similar to the one that smugly crossed Frosty's mind, doubling up with a feeling of relief. 'With Jon in attack again, along with Brian, I don't have to suffer you-know-who messing things up any more,' Frosty chuckled. 'He'll understand – he's used to it!'

Back in the changing room, Luke found himself nursing the number thirteen shirt, try-ing to come to terms with the irony of the situation.

74

'Bad luck!' Jon consoled him. 'Like old friends, you and that shirt!'

Luke nodded sadly. 'Yeah, but I thought it was about time that even the best of pals must part. Didn't want to see it again just yet.'

'Cheer up. I'll put in a good word for you with Frosty and maybe he'll bring you on at half-time on Thursday, OK?'

'Thanks, Johan,' Luke sighed. 'As long as we win, that's the main thing, I guess. Football's a team game, and a manager has to do what he thinks is right for the side.'

'It's tough at the top, eh, Luke? You know all about running a team.'

Luke forced a grin. 'Yeah,' he agreed under his breath. 'But at least on Sundays the manager makes sure his own name is the first one that goes down on the team sheet!'

'No, you can't be excused from my lesson tomorrow,' Mr Jenkins stated firmly. 'Your work is careless and untidy and you're falling behind.'

'B . . . but I'll have to miss the match if I don't get permission to leave early, sir,' Brain said, almost whimpering.

'Tough!' snapped the teacher. 'Better to miss the match, than miss maths. If I thought you'd really been trying and working hard, I might have let you go – just this once.'

'But I *have* been trying, sir,' Brain pleaded. 'It's just that . . .'

'Sorry, Brian, I've made my decision and that's final. You'll just have to inform Mr Winter that you can't play.'

Brain picked up his bag and shuffled out of the classroom, passing a smirking Matthew on the way. 'Thicko!' came the hissing taunt. 'You can't play, anyway. You're rubbish!'

Brain felt his fists clench, but fought down the urge to lash out at his tormentor. Tears prickled behind his eyes, and no way did he want Matthew to see how upset he was.

Gary had to quicken his step to catch up with Brain along the corridor. 'I heard what Jenkins said. What a—'

'Doesn't matter!' Brain cut him off. 'It's my own rotten fault getting involved again. I should have known something like this would happen.'

'It *does* matter,' Gary insisted. 'Jenkins has got no right to stop you from playing for the Comp. We need you. We've got no chance without you.'

77

Brain glanced at his friend. 'You mean that?'

'Course I do. I wouldn't have said it otherwise. Don't listen to Matt. He's just narked and taking it out on you.'

'What's *he* got to be narked about?'

'Us leaving early tomorrow and missing maths.'

'Doesn't look like I will be now.'

'We'll see about that. C'mon, let's go and find Frosty. The sooner he knows his new star player has been banned, the better!'

'Are you coming with me?'

'You bet. I want to make sure Frosty's gonna do something about it!'

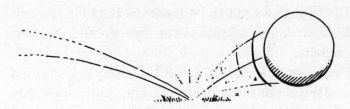

7 Debut Drama

'How did you wangle it with Mr Jenkins, sir?' asked Gary.

The footballers had clambered noisily into the school minibus for Frosty to drive them into town to play against Millbank Comprehensive.

'Easy, Gregg!' Frosty grinned wickedly.

'I'm Gary, sir. Gregg's the ugly one!'

'Ah, yes, Gary, right,' Frosty said, peering round at the twin without showing any real sign of proper recognition. 'I promised him that Brian would stay in two lunchtimes next week to catch up on the work.'

'Oh, thanks very much, sir,' grunted Brain. 'Just what I wanted.'

'Knew you wouldn't mind. Worth the sacrifice, eh?'

'I hope so. Are Millbank any good?'

Brain discovered the answer to that for himself less than a minute into his debut. Feeling nervous, he was a little slow going for Sanjay's throw out to the wing and a more determined opponent bustled him off the ball. The boy whipped a centre into the goalmouth and Millbank's tall centre-forward did the rest. He met the ball with his forehead at point-blank range and sent it hurtling into the net off the underside of the crossbar.

'Show him your fangs next time, Dracula, and he won't dare get that near you again,' muttered Tubs, booting the ball back upfield.

For once, Sanjay didn't respond to the jibe. He was still glaring out at the cowering Brain. Off the pitch, Frosty thought he was watching the start of a horror movie, fearful of the terrors that might lie ahead for his makeshift side.

'C'mon, wake up!' he bellowed at them. 'Get yourselves sorted out. If we wanted to give them a walkover, we needn't have bothered turning up.'

Swillsby were as rattled as their woodwork,

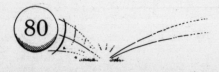

but it wasn't Frosty's rantings that finally stung them into action. Luke's touchline commentary captured the vital factor: *'Finding it a struggle without their underrated marksman, Luke Crawford, the Comp look to their new captain, cousin Jon, to steady the sinking ship. Jon controls a pass effortlessly and drifts into Millbank territory like a piece of flotsam after the early wreckage of his side's cup hopes . . .'*

Luke paused for a moment, absurdly pleased with that particular simile, but then a sudden doubt crossed his fertile mind. Was it flotsam or jetsam? He made a mental note to check the

definitions in his dictionary when he got back home. Momentarily distracted, he suddenly realized that Jon was now almost into the Millbank penalty area.

Racing along the side of the pitch, Luke picked up the theme of his commentary where he had left off: '. . . *Is the captain now going to torpedo Millbank's dreams of victory? Jon weaves his silky way past two mesmerized defenders and shoots! Sorry, no he doesn't, but he's fooled the goalie too. The boy dived, but Jon's still got the ball and now just walks it into the empty net. Pure Johan Cruyff!*'

The equalizer stunned Millbank and allowed Swillsby to enjoy the upper hand for the rest of the half. They couldn't score again, but many of their most promising moves came from Brain's skilful runs down the left wing. As his confidence increased, so did his influence on the game, and he created several chances that were squandered by his teammates.

Luke pulled off his tracksuit top during Frosty's team talk, dropping a heavy hint that he expected to be sent on for the second half. 'Keep this up, lads,' Frosty urged them. 'The goals will come.'

'Any subs yet, sir?' asked the captain pointedly.

'No need to make any changes, Jon,' Frosty insisted. 'Like the saying goes, "If it ain't broke, don't fix it!"'

Luke rezipped his top in disappointment and then saw his chances of an appearance lessen when Millbank began the second period like they had the first. Millbank's blue shirts laid siege to Sanjay's goal and the keeper took a knock on the knee as he made a desperate dive at an attacker's feet. While he was still hobbling, he conceded a second goal when the same boy burst past Big Ben to shoot high into the corner.

'Tighter, Ben, get inside his shirt!' yelled Frosty. 'Don't give him space to turn and run at you.'

Once more Swillsby weathered the storm. Their defending wasn't pretty to watch but proved effective enough, with Sanjay on top form. He produced two excellent saves to keep his team in the game, but their own attack was making little headway. Brain was being marked more tightly and not even Jon could repeat his salvage act.

The captain's dribbling forays often ended in cul-de-sacs of defenders, but one of these lone

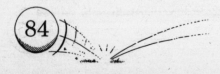

raids finally earned a free-kick when he was obstructed two metres outside the Millbank penalty area.

'Luke has all kinds of codes in this situation,' Brain grinned, 'but I can't remember any of 'em!'

'No matter.' Jon smiled back. 'My system is more simple. I pass and you shoot, OK?'

'Got it!'

On the referee's whistle, the captain rolled the ball to one side and Brain hit it with his left foot. The ball rose no more than a metre from the ground as it sped towards the goal, taking a slight deflection on the way off somebody's leg to zip past the unsighted keeper.

It was a wonderful moment for Brain. It was worth staying in every lunchtime for the thrill of scoring a goal on his school team debut and being mobbed by his delighted teammates.

Tubs lifted Brain clean off his feet in a great bear hug of congratulations. 'The equalizer! You've done it, Brain!'

'Yeah, you've really gone and done it!' added Gary, and Brain picked up the warning note in his voice.

'What do you mean?'

'Frosty will be looking for some mug to write up a match report for the school magazine.

It might be you now.'

Brain felt something squirm in the pit of his stomach, completely erasing all his excitement and pleasure. He could hardly dare trust his voice. 'I didn't know anything about this,' he squeaked.

'Don't you ever read the monthly mag?' Gary asked, and then realized that was a silly question. He saw that his friend's face, recently flushed with blood, had now drained to a ghostly white. 'Sorry, I shouldn't have said anything.'

'Too late,' the winger wheezed. 'Wish I'd gone to maths now!'

'*And there goes the final whistle,*' sighed the commentator wistfully a few minutes after Brain's goal. '*Two apiece, meaning a replay back at Swillsby, but it was hardly a classic cup tie. The unadventurous Swillsby manager, Frosty Winter, made no use of his subs. Bringing on someone like Luke Crawford might well have proven a match-winning gamble . . .*'

Luke was pleased about his protégé's successful debut, but didn't feel like joining in the boisterous celebrations back on board the bus. Brain, too, was strangely subdued, sitting quietly at the end of one of the long seats and

staring out of the gap he'd created in the steamed-up windows.

Luke leant forward and tapped him on the shoulder. 'Thought you'd have been jumping about after a performance like that. Frosty will pick you for every match now. Told you it'd all work out well, didn't I?'

Brain didn't answer, returning his attention to the darkening view outside. Luke caught Gary's eye instead. 'What's the matter? Has somebody said something to upset him?'

'Frosty!' Gary hissed. 'He's asked Brain to

write the match report for the mag to boast how well the team played.'

'I've always wanted to do that!' Luke grumbled. 'Brain's first game and he gets the job straightaway, lucky thing!'

'Don't be daft, Luke – think!' Gary snapped.

'Ah, right,' he murmured when the penny dropped. 'I see – sorry.'

He realized also why Brain felt unable to refuse. Frosty would be the last person to understand anything about his dyslexic difficulties. Luke poked Brain in the back. 'Don't worry,' he whispered. 'I'll help you . . .'

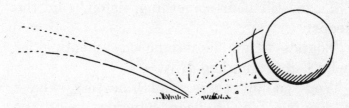

8 Foggy Fools

'We must be mad trying to play a game of football in this!' cried Tubs.

'We *are* mad!' cackled Sanjay. 'We all take after our skipper.'

Tubs peered upfield through the dense fog. 'What's going on, any idea?'

'Nope, not a clue,' said the Swifts' goalie, shaking his head. 'Last time I saw the ball was when it suddenly flew across our penalty area and disappeared again.'

'Perhaps they've already abandoned the match and forgotten to tell us!'

They laughed at such a ridiculous notion, but then looked at each other. 'Nah!' said Sanjay. 'They wouldn't go and do a thing like that – would they?'

'Maybe they don't even realize we're still out here.'

'I can still hear something, listen,' said the keeper.

'Sounds to me like somebody shouting for help!' Tubs remarked drily.

'You go up there and find out what's happening. You've been hanging about our goalmouth all match.'

'That's so I know where I am. If I wander too far away, I might never be able to find my way back again.'

'Don't be such a big coward, go on. You're playing everybody onside.'

'Huh! How can anyone tell? Ref and linesman can't see anybody more than ten metres away from them.'

As Tubs began to venture forward cautiously, he was almost trampled upon by a horde of green shirts as their opponents suddenly charged out of the fog towards the Swifts' goal.

'Sanjay!' Tubs screamed. 'They're here. Watch out!'

Sanjay was too slow to react. Without further warning, something whooshed over his head, smacked against the crossbar and rebounded out of sight once more.

'Guess that must have been the ball,' he muttered. 'Either that or a low-flying bird with a splitting headache!'

'Well left, Sanjay!' came a piping voice out of the swirling shrouds of fog. It was Luke on his way by, scampering after the ball as usual.

'Hold it a minute, Skipper!' cried Sanjay. 'This is stupid. I can't see a thing in this fog.'

'Fog?' Luke queried, looking around as if noticing it for the first time. 'Well, yes, I suppose it is a bit misty.'

'Misty! It's a double pea-souper. Get the ref to call it off, will you, and we can all go home – if we can work out which way to go.'

'Not seen the ref for a while,' Luke admitted. 'I suppose he's around here somewhere. Have you let a goal in yet?'

'Not as far as I know,' the keeper replied sarcastically.

'Good. Must still be nil–nil, then. I know we haven't scored.'

'We never do,' muttered Sanjay, but he was talking to himself. Luke had vanished,

94

swallowed up by the fog as if in a wizard's black cloak.

'He's a nutcase!' grinned Tubs.

'We know that,' agreed Sanjay. 'And I think he's getting worse.'

The referee was at the time standing near the halfway line talking to the team managers. 'No point in trying to carry on, it's getting thicker by the minute,' he told them. 'Wasn't too bad when we kicked off. At least then I could just about make out both goals from here.'

'Hoped it might lift,' said Luke's dad as Brain

dribbled past them with the ball, heading the wrong way. 'Hey! Turn round, Brain!'

The winger put his foot on the ball and halted, gave a quick grin and then set off back over the halfway line again, Luke yapping at his heels. The men just caught a snatch of the commentary. *'And there goes Brain, the Swifts' fleet-footed winger, but his skipper's not being outpaced. He's up with him in support, screaming for the ball . . .'*

Screaming for the ball and commentating is quite tricky to do at the same time, so Luke switched off his imaginary microphone. 'Pass it inside, Brain,' he yelled. 'I'm unmarked.'

'Keen, isn't he, that lad?' remarked the referee. 'The only way I've been able to locate the ball so far is to pick up his running commentary!'

'Aye, that's m'boy!' grinned Dad. 'He's always where the action is.'

As the referee jogged after the players, preparing to abandon the match, there was a sudden demented cry from somewhere deep in the fog. *'Goooaaalll!'*

The referee had to blow his whistle loudly several times to round up all of the players into the centre-circle and tell them the game was off.

'I don't believe it!' cried Luke. 'I've just gone

and scored a goal to put us in front. We need the points.'

'Sorry, lad. The game will have to be played again sometime.'

'Shame, Skip!' Dazza consoled him. 'Did you actually score?'

'Don't sound so shocked. Course I did!' said Luke. 'Long-range beauty, it was, as well. Goalie never even saw it.'

'I bet he didn't!' scoffed Sanjay. 'I know the feeling.'

'Won't your goal count now?' Brain asked.

Luke shook his head sadly. 'Not when a game gets abandoned.'

'I've got a funny feeling this goal will,' Sanjay hissed to Tubs out of the corner of his mouth. 'At least in his little black notebook!'

When everybody else had left the changing cabin, Luke and Brain sat together in the corner. 'I'll lock up, Dad,' Luke said. 'I'm just helping Brain get something sorted out, OK?'

'Fine, but if you're not back home for lunch, we'll send out a search party,' Dad joked.

Brain stared at a blank piece of paper on his lap. 'Frosty wants this report given in to him tomorrow. Guess I'll have to come up with some sort of excuse why I've not been able to do it.'

'That's no good. He'll only make you stay in and write it instead.'

'Can't. I'm already doing extra maths at lunch for Jenkins.'

'Frosty won't let you get out of it. He'll stand over you while you do it, if necessary.'

'He'll get very tired legs, then. He could stand there all week and it wouldn't make any difference. Even if he told me what to put, I couldn't spell it.'

'That wouldn't matter. With your untidy writing, Frosty wouldn't be able to read the words anyway!'

98

The boys grinned at each other. 'What am I gonna do, Skipper? I'm real stuck.'

'Leave it to me,' said Luke confidently, taking the paper out of Brain's unresisting hands. 'I know the kind of thing he's after. Frosty just wants to show Matthew and Adam that the school team doesn't need them any more.'

'But won't he realize I haven't done it? I mean, my writing's huge and all over the place. Yours is small and dead neat.'

'No problem. I'll do it on the word processor and print your name on the bottom. Dead easy to fool Frosty. He'll never know the difference!'

Brain wasn't so sure, but he had no choice. 'Guess so. At least he'll have his report and that's the main thing. Get him off my back.'

What Brain didn't know, never having read the *Chronicle*, was that everybody could spot one of Luke's football reports a mile off, even in thick fog!

Brain nipped into Frosty's empty classroom before morning registration and slapped the match report down onto the teacher's desk. He turned to make his intended quick exit but found his escape route barred.

'Not so fast, young man. Let's have a read of your effort first.'

Frosty slumped into his chair, beckoning Brain to stand by his desk as he tore open the envelope and took out the printed report. He read aloud the headline over the 2–2 scoreline: 'NEW STAR SHINES IN CUP DRAW – yes, not bad, Brian, but better perhaps to be a little bit more modest, eh?'

Brain shuffled his feet, dreading what other embarrassments might lie in wait. Luke had just slipped the sealed envelope to him at the school gate without letting on what he'd written inside.

Frosty read on. '*Swillsby's new-look Year 8 soccer team are on the cup trail. They earned themselves a home replay against Millbank Comprehensive when debutant Brian "Brain" Draper, top scorer for the Swifts, lashed home a late equalizer from a clever free-kick routine much practised by his Sunday League side . . .*'

Frosty paused to peer quizzically up at Brain. 'Did you write all this stuff yourself, Brian?'

Brain managed a little shrug. 'Well, I had a bit of help,' he confessed reluctantly, hoping that such a vague answer might suffice.

'Hmm, only giving the Swifts all this glowing

publicity wasn't perhaps quite what I had in mind for the school mag,' mused Frosty before resuming his reading. *'The powerful Millbank outfit scored early on in both halves, but keeper Sanjay Mistry pulled off a series of good saves to prevent them increasing their lead. Then it was time for new captain Jon Crawford to take centre stage. He rocked Millbank before half-time with a superb solo goal that even the great Johan Cruyff would have been proud of.'*

Brain squirmed as Frosty stared at him again. 'Ye-es, quite a lively style,' Frosty drawled in his best sarcastic tone. 'And this reference to Mr Cruyff has a certain ring to it as well . . .'

When the reddening Brain made no reply, Frosty sighed and then winced as he glanced back at the sheet and saw what was coming. *'Although the draw was a well-deserved result,'* he quoted, *'the school might even have grabbed a spectacular victory if any of the substitutes had been given the chance to play a dramatic cameo role in the closing stages.'*

Frosty stroked his chin. 'Well, quite a masterpiece, this report, Brian. You've even managed to criticize the tactics too.'

'It wasn't meant like that, sir, it was just . . .'

Frosty interrupted him. 'Surprised you failed

to mention at least one of these subs by name! What exactly is a cameo role, then?'

Brain stalled for time, struggling to come up with something that sounded similar. 'Well, er, it's a bit difficult to explain, sir . . .'

'Try, Brian, try!'

'Um, yes, it's to do with cameras, like, and . . .'

'Come on, Brian, give me some credit, please! It's got nothing to do with cameras. It's obvious you didn't write this report – but we both know who did, don't we?'

Brain gave up and nodded. 'Yes, sir.'

'That Luke Crawford's on another planet. Why did you let *him* – of all people – get his hands on it, eh? Tell me.'

Brain didn't answer, looking down at the floor, unwilling to admit to his difficulties with writing.

Frosty lost patience with the boy. 'Right, I'll give the honour to the captain now. You can come into this room at lunch and write five hundred lines: *I must never let Luke Crawford play a cameo role!*'

Brain reeled with the shock of the punishment and attempted to gabble out some words. 'Um, er, I can't . . . can't do that . . . sir . . .'

'What do you mean, you can't? You *will*! I've just told you to, lad!'

'B . . . but I've got to stay in at lunch for Mr Jenkins, sir – remember?'

Frosty suddenly pounded his desk with annoyance and jumped out of his seat, making the boy start backwards. Brain thought for a moment that he was going to be attacked.

'Right, you can also stay in at break for me,' Frosty stormed. 'Every breaktime for as long as it takes you to do those lines – if you ever want to play football for this school again!'

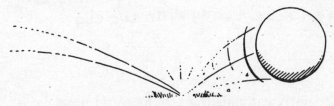

9 Cameo Role

Brain sat hunched over a table at break, facing an impossible task. He couldn't even remember the sentence he was supposed to be writing.

'Ought to make Luke do these lines for me as well,' he groaned and flung his pen at the wall in frustration. It didn't help. All it achieved was to break the pen.

Sighing, he borrowed a pencil from Frosty's desk and scribbled a short note of apology for the teacher.

This time he deliberately misspelt his name, placed the note on the desk and left the room. He

deeR miZZteR wiNteR
i am ZoRRe i kaNot do my LiNz i am Nott
veRi gud at ZqeliNg aNd ritiNg az yu kaN
Zee ZoRRe adowte tHe ReqoRte az well
                              fRom BRaiN
9.2. i Hoq tHe comq wiNz tHe cuq

felt there was nothing else he could have done.

After lunch, working in the maths room on the exercises Mr Jenkins had set him, Brain was interrupted by the arrival of Frosty. Brain had been dreading this moment, but the sports teacher was no longer angry and pulled up a chair to sit next to him.

'Why on earth didn't you tell me you're dyslexic?' Frosty began.

Brain was taken by surprise. 'How do you know that, sir?'

'I can tell from your writing now that I've seen it for the first time. And I've just had a word with your English teacher.'

'Miss Elliot doesn't know for sure. She just thinks I am.'

'I *know* you are,' stressed Frosty. 'Because I am too!'

Frosty's sudden revelation was too much to take in straightaway. 'I . . . er . . . didn't know that a teacher might be dyslexic,' Brain said lamely.

'Why not? All sorts of people are. It doesn't stop them doing their jobs properly, even if it means they might have to work harder to succeed. You don't have to let the problem hold you back.' Frosty paused and then smiled before he continued. 'I suppose that's why I can get so ratty when I see somebody else being lazy and wasting their own natural talents.'

'Sorry, sir. I didn't think you'd understand, so I hoped I might get away with it if Luke helped me out.'

Frosty nodded sympathetically. 'No doubt Luke thought he was doing the right thing, but he always tends to get too carried away. Haven't you had your dyslexia confirmed officially?'

Brain shook his head and Frosty stood up. 'Right, I'll make it my business to see that you take some tests soon that will show up exactly what your specific difficulties are.'

'What will happen after that?'

'Plenty, if I have anything to do with it, Brian.

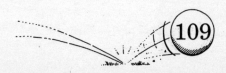

You need the kind of specialist individual teaching that I was never lucky enough to have when I was a kid. People didn't know much about dyslexia then – but they do now.'

'Thank you, sir, I didn't expect . . .'

'That's all right – and don't worry, I'll have a little word with Mr Jenkins and make sure *he* understands the situation too.'

'What about the lines, sir?'

'Forget all about those stupid things! You just concentrate on helping us to win that replay. I've fixed it up for next Saturday morning, and I want to see you flying down that wing. Right?'

'Right, sir,' Brain grinned. 'I'll be there.'

So was Luke, but again only as one of the substitutes, wearing his striped number thirteen shirt. The team was unchanged from the first match with several Swifts enjoying the bonus of another appearance for the Comp.

'Nice to be able to see the other end of the pitch after that farce last Sunday,' said Tubs.

'Yeah, and I hope the ball's up that end more than it is this,' put in Big Ben. 'Gonna be a tough game again.'

'Sure is,' Sanjay said with relish. 'So don't let's

110

give Millbank a quick goal start like before. Concentrate right from the kick-off.'

This time it was Millbank who were caught napping, their defence cut to ribbons by Gregg and Jon's interpassing. The goalkeeper looked to have Gregg's shot covered until a defender blocked it and the ball rolled into Brain's path as he followed up. The winger had the simplest tap-in goal, with the keeper left wrong-footed by the opposite post.

'*What a start!*' shrieked the commentator, almost taken unawares himself by the speed of the goal. Luke had been busy retying a broken bootlace, but now made up for lost time with a tangled string of clichés: '*One–nil! Swillsby have turned the tables on Millbank, throwing the shell-shocked visitors into the deep end and giving them a mountain to climb . . .*'

The goal gave Brain a surge of confidence and he proceeded to torture his marker, beating him easily on either side. It was looking like one of Brain's good days, and he continued to torment the opposition even after their teacher instructed a second boy to cover him as well.

Sanjay was enjoying a good day too. This was largely because he had so little to do before the interval that not even he could let a goal in. He

did try, fluffing his attempt to catch a cross, but he was saved by Big Ben's size nine boot belting the ball out of danger.

Swillsby went into half-time two goals ahead, both scored by Brain. For his second, he didn't even need to beat the two defenders. As they hesitated, not wanting to dive in with their tackles too early, Brain sensed that the keeper had strayed off his line and executed a perfect lob.

'Two–nil! An unstoppable effort from Brain into the top corner,' Luke babbled on. *'At this rate, Millbank's teacher will be dishing out lines to his players during the interval – "We must not give the number eleven any more shooting chances!" With the match so one-sided, this is a golden opportunity for Frosty to unleash his deadly subs to sink the enemy good and proper!'*

Frosty, however, was still taking no risks, especially with Luke, although Tubs did give way reluctantly to one of the other substitutes. Nearby, there was another pair of boys equally disappointed.

'Looks like the Comp's gonna win,' muttered Adam. 'We might as well clear off if we can't jeer at them losing.'

'Yeah, Millbank aren't much cop,' agreed

Matthew. 'We'd have thrashed 'em at their place if we'd still been playing.'

'Brain's running riot. Frosty's been dead lucky, Brain turning up like this after we'd packed it in.'

'Huh! Brain-less, you mean,' Matthew snorted. 'Let's heckle him a bit and put him off.'

'Thick-o! Thick-o!' they chanted, loud enough for Brain to hear, but making sure Frosty was out of range.

Brain kept looking round at them, finding it hard to ignore their continued taunts. He was also astonished to hear another voice, so familiar

yet out of context, suddenly cutting in to silence them.

'That's enough, you two! Either shut up or go home.'

It was Jenkins! Brain could scarcely believe it – and neither could his critics. Jenkins was the last person they expected to see on the touchline. He had never even been known to show any interest in football.

'C'mon, it's getting too crowded round here,' said Matthew churlishly. 'Let's go back to my place and watch the box.'

'Thanks, sir,' said Brain when he next trotted past the teacher. 'They were getting on my nerves.'

'Can't have our new star distracted, can we, Brian?' Mr Jenkins grinned. 'I've come here specially this morning to see you play.'

It was at that moment, however, when Millbank finally managed to strike back. Sanjay misjudged the pace of a shot, dived down too late and let the ball slither through his hands into the net.

Fortunately for Swillsby, Brain killed any possible fightback stone dead. Straight from the restart, Jon curled the ball out to him on the wing and Brain set off on a run, hugging

115

the touchline. He skipped past one challenge, but the second defender stepped in to do his job and knock the ball out of play.

No-one could accuse Luke's commentary of not being on the ball. *'Brain wins a throw-in and a skilful spectator – yours truly – traps the ball and flicks it straight into Gary's arms. Millbank have been caught off guard, not marking up, and Gary's long throw has put Brain in the clear. He's only got the keeper to beat. It's a narrow angle, but he shoots – and scores! Goooaaalll! Made by Luke Crawford's quick reflexes . . .'*

'Wonderful goal, Brian!' cheered Mr Jenkins. 'I'm glad to see you know all about acute angles now!'

'Brain's a hat-trick hero!' Tubs told the teacher in delight. 'He's got all our three goals.'

Their hopes raised and dashed within a minute, Millbank took it badly, arguing among themselves and looking a beaten side. Frosty checked his watch and decided he'd give Luke the final five minutes as a reward for his help at the throw-in.

'I'll let him have that cameo role he craves so much,' Frosty chuckled to himself. 'He can't do too much damage in that time.'

Famous last words. Frosty was regretting

them the moment Luke ran enthusiastically onto the pitch and tripped up over his trailing laces.

'Right wing, Luke – and stay there,' Frosty instructed him, knowing it would be in vain. The boy was so keen to get into the action, he didn't even bother tying up his laces and gave no indication of having heard.

Luke's first touch of the ball as a player on the pitch was a disaster. Inside his own half, he attempted for some reason better known to - himself to send the ball all the way back to Sanjay. His boot flew off as he made contact and the pass went astray, straight to the feet of an attacker. Sanjay was out of position and out of luck. The striker accepted his free gift gladly, lofting the ball over Sanjay into the yawning goal to leave Millbank only one goal behind again.

'Sorry, Johan,' Luke murmured as they prepared to kick off. 'Got boot trouble.'

'So I noticed,' Jon sighed. 'Just stay up front now, and let's see if we can repair the damage. Best form of defence is attack, I reckon.'

Luke grinned at his cousin. 'Dead right. I bet that's just what Johan Cruyff always says.'

Swillsby had another scare first, though, when a long, snaking cross-shot was turned round the post by Sanjay at full stretch.

'Corner, ref!' claimed Millbank loudly when Frosty gave a goal-kick.

Sanjay was a bit annoyed as well that Frosty didn't realize he had touched it. 'Typical! Best save of the game too. Would have gone in if I hadn't got my fingertips to it.'

The Millbank players were still chuntering as Brain collected the goal-kick and passed the ball inside to the captain. Frosty glanced at his watch again, horrified to see there was still another minute left. 'No chance of any injury time being added on, not with that maniac Luke on the loose,' he grimaced. 'This match is ending dead on time, if not before!'

Jon slipped the ball to Luke, but his cousin was too busy examining his laces which had come undone yet again. Even the commentary's sound was muted. 'Luke! Man on!' cried Jon.

By instinct, Luke stabbed out a foot and deflected the ball out to Gregg just before a defender could whack it away and put Swillsby under pressure again. While Gregg trundled the ball towards the corner flag to try and use up a

119

bit of time, Luke limped into the Millbank penalty area, carrying his right boot. He turned the volume back up.

'Luke Crawford battles on to the end, playing in stockinged feet as he waits hopefully for a cross from the right wing. Oh, Gregg's gone and lost control of the ball. Time to get the boot back on, just in case . . .'

Luke took his eye off the game once more to bend down, unaware that Jon had won back possession. The captain's shot was half blocked and the goalkeeper desperately lashed out with his foot to try and clear the ball before Jon could pounce on the rebound.

'Oww!'

The football struck Luke smack on the backside and ricocheted past the helpless goalie to bobble over the line. Luke was laid flat out, face down in the dirt, until Jon hoisted him to his feet.

'What a *cheeky* goal!' laughed his cousin.

Luke rubbed his sore bottom ruefully. 'Doesn't matter which bit you score with,' he grinned. 'They all count just the same!'

'Some more than others,' Jon told him. 'That one's made sure we're in the next round of the cup.'

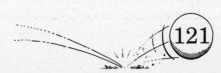

Luke sat in a happy daze in the changing room. He was looking forward to recording their 4–2 victory in his notebook and entering his own name for the first time in the list of goal scorers for the school team.

Gradually he sensed that all was not well with Brain next to him. 'C'mon, you should be over the moon, not looking as sick as a parrot,' he said as a joke. 'Frosty's going to get you extra help for your dyslexia and you've just paid him back with a hat-trick. What's up?'

'Oh, nothing really. Just Matt bugging me a bit. You don't think I'm thick, do you, Luke?'

'Course not,' replied Luke. 'Just daft, that's all.'

'Daft?'

'Yeah, football daft, like me!' Luke grinned. 'We all are!'

THE END